# The
# Hidden POrtal
# To Wren

by
*Nan C. Cataldi*

# The Hidden POrtal To Wren

### BOOK 2
### OF
### THE KEYS OF BEING TRILOGY

by

*Nan C. Cataldi*

**Cover Illustration by Mark Sean Wilson**

INKWELL BOOKS™
Writing - Publishing - Printing

ISBN: 978-1-939625-05-2


Library of Congress Control Number: 20161227968


Published by Inkwell Productions
10632 N. Scottsdale Rd, Unit 695
Scottsdale, AZ 85254-5280


Tel. 480-315-3781
E-mail info@inkwellproductions.com
Website www.inkwellproductions.com

*Printed in the United States of America*

# DEDICATION

For my sister, who continues to inspire me. Though she has struggled with MS for more than twenty-five years, she is ever optimistic and enthusiastic about life.

# TABLE OF CONTENTS

CHAPTER 1

# IN THE DESERT

Behind the invisible veil in the tranquil world of Wren, perched on a marble bench near her palace sanctuary, was the tall, supernatural, majestic ruler of Wren, Glymirra. With the upper body, head and arms of a human-like giant and the wings and lower body of a white eagle, she was given the charge as Keeper of the Balance and Caretaker of all the Living on Gaeya, except for humans. Patiently she waited for her two most trusted spirit creatures called Fae-rens, to return from Gaeya, with the Elka, one of the Keys of Being that is needed to maintain the balance. It was lost for more than seventy-five years, and recovered by a ten-year old boy. Uniting the Keys would heal the land from the destruction created during the Great Second War and continues. It has caused the land to experience increased environmental devastation. Colossal earthquakes are happening all over the world; sleeping volcanoes erupting and wiping out entire lands. Many large forest fires are encroaching on cities and taking away animal habitats. Several extreme tsunamis had killed or displaced thousands of whales, dolphins and fish, coating hundreds of coastal communities with their bodies. Even a few Sea Fae-rens had lost their lives trying to save these creatures.

The leader of the dark sorcerers, Fellon, took advantage of the environmental chaos to increase his evil hold on the land.

On Gaeya (Earth), in the Kirkland's backyard two Fae-rens prepared to return to Wren. Brin-dah took the amber Key of Being and placed it in the pocket of her knee length toga. Then turned to Der-rex and said, "We need to hurry back with the Elka. Since the Evil One's sorcerers and bewitched animals have failed this time to secure the Key, I fear he will try to stop us himself. I do not know if we are quick enough or strong enough to fight him."

The two of them joined hands, then closed their eyes to call upon the warm wind to carry them. When Der-rex touched the small orb of time that hung around his neck, a great, warm gust of swirling wind gathered them up. They began traveling swiftly back through time, heading toward the veil of Wren to return the Elka to Glymirra. Without warning, they felt a tremendous pressure, like something was closing in around them, then a forceful push, which caused them to tumble violently out of control. It was as if a huge hand tried to grab them, but they were thrown into space, disrupting their travel route. As the force engulfed them, the two Fae-rens grabbed on to one another as tight as they could to keep from separating. They spun around and around in empty space, until with a powerful jolt, they halted in dead air and fell to the sandy ground with a great thud. Shocked by what had just happened, they laid on the ground next to each other, dazed for a moment.

Looking at Der-rex, Brin-dah wondered, "What happened? Are you harmed? "

"I am not sure." He paused for a moment. "It felt like

we tumbled so far. I am still weak...but unhurt."

Brin-dah stood up and began to pace. "We are not yet in Wren. Where are we? This cannot be! We need to get back. Glymirra and Gaeya need the Elka's help now! It has been too long since Gaeya has had stability."

"Please calm down Brin-dah. You must concentrate. We are alright and we still have the Elka. It is more important that we find a place to hide, before we are discovered and captured. I think the Evil One knows we have the Key."

Der-rex got to his feet with great effort, reached over and grabbed Brin-dah's hand to reassure her. He started to look around for a place to hide.

"This particular area does not look familiar. But the landscape and the cacti look similar to the desert place where Nicky lived. Maybe we can find a place to hide in those nearby mountains, until we determine when and where we are."

He paused for a moment to scan the area again. "We could not have gone very far, geographically. We only traveled a few blips before our journey was interrupted."

Brin-dah, who was always the optimistic one, now looked lost and defeated. Der-rex knew that saving this world rested on them returning the Elka. They were so close. He put his arm around her and tried to conceal his fear, but deep down he was petrified. She looked at him with a weak smile as they floated on a soft breeze, closer to a small range of mountains, trying to use their powers sparingly, as to not give away their position.

"Look over there," Der-rex pointed. A few yards away he noticed a small, narrow opening in the first mountain they approached. He let go of Brin-dah and edged slowly toward the opening. Peering in, he saw a small, deep cavern. "We can hole up in here, while we find out where we are, and see if it is safe to try and return to Wren. Somehow we must get the Elka to Glymirra."

The two of them hurried inside the low-roofed cave. As they entered, the Fae-rens joined hands, closed their eyes, and sealed the opening with their magic. The cave opening became a wall of solid rock, as if the entrance never existed. Der-rex swayed a little as he sat down on the dirt floor, the simple task exhausting him. Brin-dah touched his shoulder as she sat down next to him.

"You must rest awhile. You are still weak from the

sorcerer's spell that nearly stopped your existence when we went to rescue Nicky's dog and Molly."

Der-rex saw the stress in Brin-dah's face and whispered, "We both just need a little time to rest, and figure out a way back to Wren before the Evil One discovers where we are hiding."

At the same time, a non-magical worker Fae-ren named Tan-na who had followed the two protector spirits to Gaeya, returned to Wren with the Sentinels. When they arrived, Glymirra received them immediately.

"Where are Brin-dah and Der-rex?" she asked.

"Brin-dah said they would be right behind us," replied Tan-na. "They should be here very soon. They are bringing you the Elka."

But a long time passed and the two Fae-rens did not appear. Glymirra sent the hawks, her Sentinels, to help the centaur, Kendar, guard the portals into outer Wren, until she could find out why her two most trusted spirit creatures had not returned. Something was amiss.

"Where can they be?" Tan-na said with great distress.

"Brin-dah told me that she had the Key, and she and Der-rex were leaving the future to return here." Tan-na turned then sat down on a nearby marble bench just inside the gates of the inner realm. Hanging her head in despair and thinking too many bad things had happened. Then all of a sudden, she jumped up and stated in a positive voice "But Brin-dah is strong and has powerful magic. She must be alright," Trying to convince herself.

However, Glymirra sensed that all was not well for her Fae-ren Protectors.

"Something must have happened to them during their travel. I must consult the Reflection of Ages. If Brin-dah and Der-rex are still on Gaeya, it will find their location."

The Keeper of the Balance hurried back to her sanctuary to consult the future. Looking into the very large smooth, sapphire-colored crystal, which hung on the wall of her chambers, she commanded, "Show me Brin-dah and Der-rex." First a mist appeared around the Reflection of Ages. As it cleared, Glymirra saw her two Protector Fae-rens huddled together in a cave in the same arid place she had sent them. She was somewhat relieved to see that they were alright and still in possession of the Key that glowed in Brin-dah's pocket. But what was strange, is that they had moved a few years further into the future. *How did this happen?* Glymirra looked again into the crystal to see the vast destruction all over Gaeya. She closed her tennis ball-size, blue eyes then waved her hand over the sapphire crystal. Using her mind, she sent a form of her body through time to the cave where Der-rex and Brin-dah were hiding. Brin-dah and Der-rex trembled at the vision. Appearing in front of the resting Fae-rens was a faint form of their ruler, the Grand Glymirra. They had never known the Keeper of the Balance to transcend in this manner.

"Do not fear my image. I came to give you information. But first, you must tell me what happened to you as you began your journey back to Wren."

Der-rex was too weak to speak, so Brin-dah explained about the huge, forceful hand that attempted to grab them, and how the two of them spun out-of-control and landed with a jerk. "We were afraid to travel so soon, in case the evil was still nearby."

"This explains how you two ended up five years further into the future. The hand is that of the Evil One, who now calls himself Fellon the Cursed or the Cursed One. He knew you would be leaving to go to Wren as soon as you touched the Elka. It is very frightening and quite strange, but the evil seems to know a Fae-ren's every move. It is time that I send spies to get me more information about this Fellon. For now, you must enlist the help of a human to return the Key. Now you will...."

Without warning the ground began to shake violently and loose rocks showered down on Brin-dah and Der-rex. The Fae-rens were stunned as they were covered in dust and debris. The tremors continued for five solid minutes.

Glymirra noticed their surprised expressions and explained, "You are in the future now, where Gaeya is experiencing more and more volatile behavior. The plates under this planet's crust are shifting farther and faster than ever before. Dormant volcanoes are erupting on every land mass. Several large islands have sunk into the seas, covered by waves taller than the oldest sequoia trees. Fires are burning in many of the forests. Ice caps are moving south and turning the tropical lands into frigid areas. Even the humans are beginning to sustain losses. The evil is everywhere, taking advantage of the havoc. The Fae-rens can barely keep up with protecting the animals and plant life. Therefore, I am reluctant to send you any help at this moment. You must do this on your own. I am afraid if too many Fae-rens are discovered in the desert, then the Cursed One may become suspicious and send even more sorcerers to thwart you. We must be careful.

"Brin-dah, do you still hold in your possession the gold opulan that you found on the boulder years ago? It is of the utmost importance that you find the young human who retrieved the Elka. You will need to give the gold opulan to him. Nicky is older now. Since I do not have a Guardian in this area, he must become the Guardian. No one else can be trusted with our secrets during these dangerous times. With his help and the help of the Elka, he will be able to return the Key to Wren through a secret portal."

In an instant, a strange- looking, large green oak leaf magically appeared in front of the two Fae-rens. "Take this map of the portal that is nearest to your location. It is in an old abandoned copper mine very close to where you now rest. This map will direct Nicky to the opening of the mine.

The opulan will take him to the correct shaft and point the way to the portal he must enter."

The ground began to shake once more, several small rocks showered down and dust filled the air around the two Fae-rens. They glanced at each other and then back to the image of Glymirra.

"Does the Cursed One," Brin-dah gulped, "know we are...in this cave?" she asked, in a quivering voice.

Glymirra smiled in reassurance. "Fear not. I do not believe so. Gaeya is so unstable in the future, the tremors are increasing everywhere. At least you are in an area that has not been ravaged like the northern and coastal areas. Without the Elka the destruction will continue to get worse, eventually affecting the desert land where you are. Possessing all the Keys of Being and placing them in the Altar will repair the balance and weaken all the great evil that has grown around us. Fellon may be aware of this, and that is why he is so desperate to stop you from returning the last Key.

"Know this, you are only seventy-five mortal miles northwest of Nicky's dwelling. Do not travel by orb and use the warm, fast wind prudently, unless it is the only way. The evil is watching. He will be looking for signs of magic. Since you are invisible, use the humans for transportation. You are not far from a main road that will take you to the human's highway and on to your destination.

"It has been five years since the Cursed One has sought Nicky. I do not think he will expect the boy to aid you. However, you may need to secure and hide the Elka. It will make you less vulnerable to the evil Fellon's sorcerers if you come into contact. I suspect that they are focused more on the Key than on Fae-rens at this time. This will give you an edge over them and time to contact Nicky. You two must remain vigilant of all the dangers that lay before you. Stay close together. You know you are stronger that way. Make sure to maintain your invisible Fae-ren forms. Nicky will remember. I have been monitoring his development. He has grown into a strong, intelligent, and noble, young man."

Glymirra's form began to flicker and fade. Brin-dah and Der-rex reached out as if to hold on to her. "But, Grand One..."

Glymirra's voice began to weaken to a whisper, "Be careful, but hurry. All...will...not...wait...long." These were the last words spoken as she disappeared from their view.

Brin-dah nervously spouted, "I am worried by this new task we must perform. I hope we are the best ones to carry it out." She was thinking how inadequate their powers were compared to the Cursed One's power. But she and her mate were created to protect--that was their job. She closed her eyes for a moment to clear the doubt and push back the fear. "Glymirra is depending on us," she announced in in a determined voice.

She turned to Der-rex and asked, "How are you feeling? We need to begin our mission."

He lifted his head toward her and smiled tiredly. "I am much better now."

"I know you are weary, but it is important that we leave here soon and head to Nicky's house. I also think it would be wise to hide the Elka here. With a few enchantments and the thick rock to hide its glow, it should be safe until we return. Since we are near a road, we can just float on the breeze there. It should not take us long to attach ourselves to a moving vehicle."

The two of them hid the Elka in a small crevice in

a dark corner of the cave. Weaving their magic through the air with their hands and whispering the magical word, "Consella," they sealed the amber key into its hiding place. For now, the Key would be safe from evil hands.

Brin-dah unsealed the cave and the two joined hands to reseal the opening, providing additional protection for the Key. Then the Fae-rens closed their eyes and waited for the warm wind they summoned. They felt the first tendrils of wind and grabbed on to it, riding it to the nearby highway. Using their thoughts to communicate to each other, they spotted a maroon pick-up truck heading in the southeast direction. As it slowed down to take the ramp onto the highway, they joined hands and landed softly in the empty bed of the truck. The truck sped down the highway, and the Fae-rens began to plan their course of action.

"We must decide how we will approach Nicky about becoming a Guardian." Looking a little upset, she whispered, "If he refuses us, all will be lost."

Der-rex touched Brin-dah's hand with his, "Remember, Brin-dah. Nicky is older now, I am sure he will understand the importance of the quest he must undertake."

Brin-dah looked into Der-rex's eyes, hesitated, then nodded in agreement.

The two of them sat in the back of the truck watching the sunset and hoping that all would go well in the morning.

CHAPTER 2

# THE NEW GUARDIAN

Fifteen year old Nicky had just caught a pass and his thin, six foot frame headed toward the goal line. "Run! Run!" he heard his teammates yell. "Touchdown!" He was the fastest player on the field. Since his experience with the Elka five years ago, no one made fun of him anymore. He was the youngest starter on the varsity football team. In fact, he was very popular at Coyote High School.

"Great job, Nick," his coach shouted. The practice game ended with a win for his team, and the other players patted his back as they ran past him to reach the end of the field. They would all meet there to get the final pep talk from their coach.

"I am very pleased. You all played well today.

Practice tomorrow at the same time. Remember, we play the Thunderbirds this Saturday. I hear they have some new guys, and they are 5 and 0. Our scouts say they are tough, and if we can win this one we'll be in line for the State playoffs. Okay, boys, shower-up!"

The team left the field and headed to the locker room. Nicky was so happy. His life had changed tremendously in the last five years. His mom was now engaged to his friend, Police Officer Michael Montoya. Molly, who now lived permanently with Mrs. Grey, was not only a good friend but now his girlfriend. At school he played sports and was well liked. He seldom thought about his previous handicaps, the damaged left leg and stammering speech which he incurred from his car accident at the age of six. It was like he had been stuck in a bad dream and then woke-up to this wonderful, problem free life.

In the locker room while a clean Nicky changed back into his jeans, he was approached by a tall, two hundred -seventy pound teen. His name was Jake. He was one of the team's best tackles and Nicky's friend.

"Hey, Nick, you want a ride home?"

"Sure, I just need to get my duffle bag. If I don't let my mom wash these dirty, sweaty clothes, they'll stand on their own." He stuffed the bag with the dirty clothes from his locker, then swung the long bag over his shoulders , put on his blue denim ball cap, leaving his dark curls hanging out, and headed out to Jake's car. Jake was a senior who lived one block from Nicky.

Nicky jumped in the car, put on his seat belt and smiled, "Home, James, I mean, Jake" then he laughed. Jake shook his head and pulled out of the parking lot, heading toward home.

"Wow, Nick! That was an awesome run at the end!"

"Yeah, I guess I ran about fifty-five yards for that touchdown. I sure hope I can do that well on Saturday. You heard Coach Reid. The Thunderbirds are the team to beat."

"I can't believe that we are in the running for State," Jake interjected as he drove. "It's the first time for our school."

"Really?" Nicky said in a surprised voice.

"Yep."

Nicky looked over at Jake. "Well, I am excited, but

that info really puts the pressure on us for Saturday's game."

"Yeah, but if we win, we will be making history!"

"It sounds really awesome, when you put it that way."

Jake pulled up to the curb next to Nicky's house. "Thanks for the ride, Jake." But as Nicky got out and closed the car door, the ground began to shake. He paused and waited for the earth to stop rumbling. "Well, I hope these tremors that we've been having don't affect our game."

Jake sort of laughed. "Oh, we'll be fine. See ya tomorrow, Nick." He waved and drove off.

Nicky knew that Arizona had been lucky when it came to earthquakes. He remembered that just last year a large portion of San Francisco's coast was lost into the ocean. He just could not understand what was happening to the Earth. Five years ago the Elka, one of the Keys of Being which had been lost, was returned to the Fae-rens. The Keys, when united, would return the Earth to an environmental balance. *Why was the balance getting worse? Why was the world experiencing so many devastating disasters? It was like a nightmare!*

He stopped for a few seconds, then shook his head and

put the happening behind him. Nothing was going to ruin his excitement about the football game on Saturday. *Absolutely nothing,* he thought. He must be very positive and concentrate on playing the game against such a tough team.

Nicky walked up to the front door. He heard Punkin whining. "I'm home, girl." He stepped into the house and petted his dog Punkin as she sat wagging her tail.

His mom watched the news with great interest. Another huge earthquake had hit the United States, this time on the northeast coast, damaging large sections of New York City and the Boston area. The Empire State Building lost the two top floors. Fortunately, only minor injuries were reported. A tsunami hit the coast of West Africa causing severe damage and loss of life. Japan experienced another intense earthquake. In shock from all the bad news from around the world of the escalating environmental disasters, Claire heard the door open and left the den. She tried to put on an optimistic face as she approached her son.

Hoping for some good news, Claire asked Nicky, "So, how was practice?"

"Great! We may be in line for the State Championship

if we win Saturday."

"Wow, that's exciting," she responded.

"But can I eat now? I'm really hungry, Mom."

"I knew you would be." She laughed and gave him a plate of meatloaf and potatoes that he devoured in a few minutes.

"Oh, Mom, here are the stinky clothes from my locker."

Claire turned and glared at him. "Please put them in the washer. I'll take care of them later. Besides I'm not sure I even want to touch them. The smell was really horrible the last time you brought them home."

"Sorry, Mom, " He wrinkled up his nose as he threw the rank smelling clothes into the wash machine.


It was about seven P.M. when the truck left the highway and entered the residential area close to where Nicky lived. Brin-dah and Der-rex exited the bed of the truck and floated toward Cactus Flower Lane. They arrived at Nicky's house that evening, just as Nicky returned from football practice. The Fae-rens saw him open the door and enter the house. The two of them would spend the night behind the Kirkland's house concealed in the backyard, behind the bushes that now formed a hedge along the back fence. There they would plan their mission. Brin-dah sat next to Der-rex and expressed her enthusiasm in making Nicky a Guardian.

"I know Nicky will be honored to become a Guardian. Only a few special humans have been given the privilege to go between the two realms, since their existence on Gaeya. He must accept this great gift that the Grand Glymirra is bestowing on him. Tonight, while he sleeps, I will remind him of the danger he faced and will face again. Then in the morning we will approach him."

Nicky finished homework then went to bed as usual. He was very tired, but for some reason that night, he had trouble falling asleep. When he at last gave-in to his exhaustion, he dreamt of magic, the Fae-rens and being chased by bewitched dogs and evil sorcerers.

When he woke-up in the morning, Nicky laid in bed going over and over in his mind how strange his dreams were during the night. He had not thought about his run-in with that evil guy's sorcerer or those possessed animals, or even

Brin-dah and Der-rex, since it all happened five years ago. *What has changed?* Then he threw his hands up, lifted his head high, and opened his eyes wide as if to rid his mind of these thoughts. He needed to focus. He had an important test this morning and then the pep rally this afternoon. The whole school would be there rooting for his team to win Saturday's game. He was so proud to be part of it. Maybe he was thinking of the Fae-rens because they gave him his life back, like it was before the car accident. Yes, that's why he was dreaming of them. That's the only explanation. He dressed, ate breakfast and left for school.

Nicky was smiling as he waved to his neighbor Mr. Rosenelli, who was sitting on his front porch drinking his morning coffee, before starting his day.

"Good Morning, Nick," Mr. R Yelled.

Nicky continued walking toward the bus stop, when a small brown wiener dog sat down in front of him. He paused as he looked at the dog. A look of shock and surprise covered his face. "Is...that...you, Der-rex?"

"Yes, I was hoping you would remember me." The little dog wagged his tail as he spoke.

"What are you doing here? I don't have anything anyone wants, do I?" Nicky asked in a confused voice.

"No, Nicky. I am here because I need your help."

"My...help! You have supernatural powers. I'm just me. I don't see how I could help you."

Then Brin-dah appeared as the young homeless woman he saw five years before.

"You're here, too," Nicky asked in a disbelieving voice.

"Yes, we have come here to bestow on you the greatest honor any human can ever attain." She reached into her jeans pocket and pulled out a gold disk, then showed it to Nicky.

"What's that?"

"It is called an opulan, a tool to open a portal in the Veil, which will take you into the outer perimeter of Wren. The Grand Glymirra made it from solid gold and embossed the cover with her wing emblem. It is the only way a human can pass thru the Veil and enter the outer circle of Wren. A human Guardian is given possession of it, so he or she can pass important information to Glymirra during times of war or great destruction. The Guardians named it the Watch of

Wren, because it looks similar to a human's pocket watch. We want you to be our new Guardian and help us return the Elka to Glymirra."

"Wait. What?! But you returned it five years ago," Nicky interrupted. "Although, I wonder why the natural disasters around the world have increased since you left. You told me that returning the Key would make things on Earth better."

"It does and it will! But we were stopped by the Evil One on our way back to Wren and thrust five years into the future. The Evil One, who is now calling himself Fellon the Cursed, knew that we had the Elka. He is doing all he can to prevent us from taking it to Glymirra in order to restore the balance. He knows that it will weaken his powers significantly. It may even cause him to lose control over all the dark ones he has under his command.

"Since he has obtained the knowledge of our travel habits, he has been tracking us and other Fae-rens. The Cursed One's sorcerers have already destroyed some of the Protector Fae-rens. We have lived since our creation for thousands of years. No Fae-ren had ever been destroyed until our leader,

Phan-non, who was captured and destroyed by Hitler's dark sorcerers during the Second Great War. But now we have lost many Fae-rens by the hand of the dark sorcerers, and Fellon has even gone so far as to threaten our world, Wren. We can no longer use the orb to return to the past and to Wren— it is not safe. It is how we can be tracked by the evil. We cannot return the Elka to Glymirra without risking discovery or losing the Key. This is why we need your help. He will not suspect you. He and his evil followers have not contacted you in the last five years. You know some of our secrets, and you have great honor and virtue. There is no other human we would trust with this task." Brin-dah pleaded, "Please...you must help us."

Nicky was still reeling from seeing Brin-dah and Der-rex again. He could not process what they were asking. "But I'm on my way to school. I have a test that I have to take, and I have an important football game coming up. I'm sorry, I know the Elka healed me, but I can't leave here right now. Too much is at stake." Just then a huge tremor shook the ground almost knocking Nicky down. "Whoa!"

"See Nicky, Gaeya is becoming more and more

unstable. All the disasters humans are experiencing are due to the loss of the Key. We cannot wait much longer. Please... you are the only one that can help us."

Nicky set his backpack down, took off his ball cap, and stood there thinking. "You need me...right now?"

"Yes. It is imperative that the Key is restored to the underground Altar of Hope by Glymirra before Gaeya is in ruins or before the Evil One discovers the underground Grotto and destroys the Altar. This would make it impossible to reunite all the Keys. The Evil One has been searching for it for many years, trying to find its location. He thinks that the purity and goodness that it possesses will emit an aura like the ones that surrounds the Grand Glymirra and all the Fae-rens. But it is so well protected that only the Keeper of the Balance knows the location of the Grotto. Still, the Evil keeps vigilant, hoping that something or someone will give away its location."

Once again the ground under Nicky shook. This time it knocked him down.

He quickly stood up, brushed off his behind, and then stared for a moment at the two Fae-rens thinking, *Wow! These tremors are getting stronger. Fast.*

"I think I see the big picture." Nicky said frowning. He took in a deep breath, calling upon all his strength, then stated, "I will...help you." He hung his head as he kicked a small rock with his foot and acknowledged, "I know this is very important. The whole...world ...needs...my help," Nicky said, as he began to grasp the enormous importance of Brin-dah's request. Feeling a little uncomfortable about his role in helping the Fae-rens, he threw up his hands. "But I'm just an ordinary, teenage boy. I hope this Glym...what's her name?"

"The Grand Glymirra."

"Yes, Glymirra. She really thinks I can be this... Guardian? What do I know about saving the world?"

"Yes, Nicky." Brin-dah touched Nicky's arm and spoke," She knows how brave you are and so do we. Der-rex would not be here if it wasn't for your courage and thoughtfulness. Now, we must find a secure place to discuss our plan."

Nicky picked up his backpack, put on his hat, and then walked them to a small nearby pavilion, a block from his house.

"This is not safe enough," Der-rex said in a criticizing voice. "It is still too open. Remember we are being hunted by the Evil One. He has spies everywhere. They know we are the last ones to possess the Key."

Then Brin-dah noted, "But we hid the Elka. Since he has all his wicked sorcerers and bewitched animals focused on finding it, I am hoping it will slow them down and give us a little more time to execute a plan that will get the Elka to Wren quicker. But I agree with Der-rex, we need to find a safer place to discuss this."

## CHAPTER 3

# THE BUTTE

The three of them paused to contemplate a discreet haven to enlighten Nicky of the dangerous course of action he must take in order to deliver the Key to Wren.

Der-rex smiled at Brin-dah and exclaimed, "I think ...we should go to Black Spirit Butte. They would be surprised to find us hiding out in such a negative place."

Brin-dah's face lit up. "Der-rex, you are a genius," She said in an excited voice. "They won't be looking for us there!"

"But what if some of the Evil One's helpers are there?" Nicky interjected.

Brin-dah smiled. "We can find out. Right, Der-rex?"

"Of course!"

Nicky stood there looking confused, as Brin-dah and Der-rex joined hands, closed their eyes and concentrated. A few seconds later the Fae-rens opened their eyes.

"You will be happy to know that no evil being inhabits any of the caves there at present. However, the butte is still shrouded in fog, and strong tremors continue to pass through it.

"Now, what is the quickest way for you to get there, Nicky?" Brin-dah asked.

"Well I'm not old enough to drive a car, so I guess I'll take the city bus." Nicky pointed down the street to the bus stop sign.

"We have to be careful traveling, so we will join you in our Fae-ren forms."

The three of them proceeded toward the bus stop. A few minutes later the bus rounded the corner. Nicky and the Fae-rens climbed on and were on their way.

As soon as Nicky sat down, he pulled out his cell phone and texted his mom.

Mom, with Brin-dah and Der-rex ... will be gone a few days

Don't worry. Tell Molly I'm OK.  B in a dead zone. C U soon

Nicky shut off his cell phone and shoved it into the side pocket of his backpack, awaiting his destination.

It wasn't long before the bus arrived at the stop close to the Butte.

"We have to walk the rest of the way," Nicky whispered to the Fae-rens.

"You walk fast and Der-rex and I will float alongside you."

"Oh, I forgot, you don't really walk." Nicky replied. He turned around to make sure they were alone, and then walked very fast toward Black Spirit Butte.

Soon he arrived at a large orange sign which stood near the base of the butte:

## DANGER
## ROCK SLIDES- KEEP OUT

He stopped and looked around for any evidence of a police cruiser. Nick had heard from some of the guys at school that the police had been patrolling the butte to keep out the teenage gangs they caught trashing the terrain along the base of this small, but treacherous mountain.

I hope no one saw me come this way, he thought to himself. Looking around once again, he spoke to the Fae-rens, "The kids know that most people are afraid of the ominous sights and sounds that come from the butte. So some of the gangs come to drink and party behind the foot of the butte, where the rock slides are. The police arrest anyone they see here."

Brin-dah heard his concerns and floated next to Nicky's ear. She whispered, "We need to use as little magic as possible, so we do not bring attention to ourselves, but we will protect you, if there is a need."

Soon they reached the front of Black Spirit Butte.

Nicky looked up and sighed. He was remembering the last time he stood at this very spot. He was ten years old and his best friend and dog were held hostage by an evil sorcerer in one of the butte's caves. All worked out for the best, but now he was here again, hoping it was under his terms not the Evil One's. He began to climb. All the recent tremors had loosened even more rock than last time, making it almost impossible to gain ground. He was strong, but he would take a few steps up, then slide down the front of the butte. This happened several times. Nicky was making very little progress. It was taking longer than he expected. In frustration, he decided to yell for help, "Hey guys, can you give me some help?" Der-rex and Brin-dah were almost to the ledge where three cave openings presented themselves, when they heard him. So they turned and floated down to Nicky.

"We are sorry. We forget you do not move like a Fae-ren," Brin-dah said in an apologetic tone. Then Der-rex grabbed his left arm while Brin-dah took hold of his right arm. They floated him up to the ledge with them and set him down in front of the largest cave opening.

"Thanks for the help. It might have taken me another

one or two more hours to reach here," he said as he dusted off his jeans. "Now what?"

"Well, Nick......" The whole butte began to tremble. Then rocks and dust began to fall. Nicky covered his head with his hands and ran inside the largest opening for shelter. The Fae-rens followed him. It was a few minutes before the huge tremor stopped.

"Wow, that was scary," Nicky said as he breathed a sigh of relief, then took of his ball cap and dusted it off.

"The Butte seems to be a little more active than before. I thought that we were goners. What if we became trapped here?"

"Remember, Nicky, that we are here with you. Our magic will help protect you in times of danger," Brin-dah touched his shoulder to calm him.

Then all of a sudden she transformed into the young homeless woman with the torn shirt and holey blue jeans. She smiled at Nicky. "Der-rex will light the way and I will walk with you to ease your mind, while we find a safe place to discuss our plan."

It was slow moving through the cavern. The opening

was large, but as they progressed further, the ceiling became lower and the walls narrower. It became a very twisted, curvy tunnel. Nicky had to stoop to move through it. His back was feeling strained from the arched position. A shiver ran down his spine. Moving through this tunnel once again reminded Nicky of the last time he had entered a cave in this butte. He was smaller then and able to navigate the tunnel of the other cave better. The teen was very uncomfortable and growing impatient. It seemed like hours since they entered the cave.

"Are we there yet?" Nicky yelled to Der-rex, who led the way deeper and deeper into the cavern.

"Yes. Yes! There are even places to sit. It looks like someone was here long, long ago."

Nicky's anxiety eased as he entered the large, open area and could stand-up to his full height again. Brin-dah walked in behind Nicky and smiled in relief. "Der-rex, this is very suitable to our need. Now we can all rest and discuss a way to get you safely into Wren with the Elka."

The room of the cavern was very large and spacious. It was well preserved like someone had lived there and left in a hurry. Slabs of rocks were laid to represent a primitive table and flat-headed boulders served as stools. A few broken clay pots lay close to a hollowed-out part of the cave wall, and in the center of the room remnants of ashes and twigs from a fire still remained. Der-rex changed into a young man and sat down on the boulder next to Nicky. Brin-dah sat across from them.

"It is important that I explain more about the parts Guardians have played in keeping the world safe. More than two thousand years ago, when some of the greatest civilizations began conquering other humans and expanding their culture and ideas, they also began disrespecting the land and other living entities. Gunpowder was introduced, causing much destruction. So, our great leader, the Grand Glymirra, enlisted a handful of humans who wanted to protect the land with all the living flora and fauna. These humans were trusted with the knowledge about our world and the importance of maintaining the balance of your world. The Guardians were given the gold opulan so that in times of great conflict, they could enter a special portal and report on the devastation and pending dangers to Glymirra. Each Guardian would then choose a descendent he trusted to carry on this work. Unfortunately, some Guardians died before they were able to pass on the knowledge of the opulan and the invisible world of Wren to the next generation. After the last Great War ended, Glymirra was hoping harmony would return to Gaeya, and she would not need to replace some of the Guardians. But as you can see, a terrible evil has grown instead. Not being able to heal the land after the Great War ended, is taking its toll on your world. The Guardians have helped protect your world in the past. Now you will help protect it as a new Guardian."

"Tomorrow we will go to the cave where the Elka is hidden. It is not far from here. We shall collect the Key and then Der-rex and I will take you to a place where we will await the rotation of Gaeya to align with one of the portals into Wren. You see, we can enter from anywhere using our magic and the orb, but a human can only enter through special portals or doorways. Their locations change, according to the movements of Gaeya around the great star sun."

"So why can't you come with me? Wouldn't it be easier if you were with me?"

"We must stay on Gaeya and make sure that the evil does not discover this secret. While you are preparing to enter the portal, we will create a diversion, so you are protected. It should give you time to enter Wren without conflict.

As the three of them talked about their plan to return the Key, Jake and some of the other teens on the football team where wondering what happened to Nicky. He hadn't shown up for his classes or for the pep rally. That wasn't like him. While the team sat on the chairs lined up on the gym floor in front of the whole school assembly, and the cheerleaders started to cheer, Coach Reid walked over to Jake and asked in a whisper, "Where is Nicky?"

"I don't know coach. I haven't seen him all day. His girlfriend Molly texted me. She is worried, too. She hasn't been able to get a hold of him either."

"Well, I sure hope he shows up for tomorrow's game. We need him! If we lose tomorrow, our chances of going to state might be lost."

Feeling let down, the coach bowed his head in despair as he walked away and sat down behind the team.

## CHAPTER 4

# THE KIRKLAND HOME

It was 4:30. Clare Kirkland's shift at the Mini Medical Clinic was over. She opened her locker and heard the beep coming from her purse. She pulled out her purse, reached in and snatched out her cell phone. As she walked to her car she saw that she had a text from Nicky. *Maybe he has some extra football practice tonight,* she thought. But then she opened the text. She was shocked to read the message, stating Nicky was with Brin-dah and Der-rex. That was not good news. What was going on? It was frightening to think that she would be unable to reach him for a few days.

As soon as Michael Montoya pulled up in his police cruiser at the Kirkland home, Claire came out running. She began to tell Michael about the text she received from Nicky.

He could tell that she was really worried. He stepped out of the cruiser and gave her a hug.

"Michael, I don't understand why the Fae-rens are here or why they need Nicky's help. It doesn't make...any... sense," she said in a shaky voice while she looked into Michael's eyes.

"Claire, dear, I don't know what to tell you, since I don't know what's going on. But I do know that Brin-dah and Der-rex will take very good care of Nicky. We must trust them and Nicky. Your son is a very smart young man. I am sure he won't do anything to jeopardize his well-being."

"I am so glad you are here, Michael. I don't think I could handle this by myself. I guess I better call Molly and tell her what's going on and not to worry. She called me when I was at work, several times, very upset that she could not get a hold of Nicky, and left three messages. I hope she understands that I do not know any more than what Nicky told me. It scares me to think that he will be unreachable!" Claire stated as she stood there trembling. Michael stepped closer and hugged her, then kissed her cheek. "Please have faith. I know he will come out of this fine. The Fae-rens will see to it."

As they sat down to dinner, they heard a knock at the front door.

"I'll get it," Michael said, as he stood up from the table.   Claire looked at him and grimaced. She wasn't expecting company.   He opened the door. It was a nervous looking, Molly.

"It's Molly," he hollered to Claire. "Come in."

The two of them entered the kitchen.

"Sorry, Molly. I haven't had time to call you back," Claire said, seeing the worried look on the teen's face.

"Is Nicky here? Is he okay?" a sad Molly asked. "Everyone at school was upset that he did not show for the pep rally or football practice. The big game is tomorrow. He never misses practice!"

"Nicky is not here, Molly. Please sit down and I will explain all I know."

A bewildered Molly pulled out a chair, and sat down.

"Nicky is with Brin-dah and Der-rex. I do not know why, but it must be important. He left me a text message, saying he would be gone for a few days. He is in a dead zone, no cell phone reception, so we cannot contact him, but he is alright as far as we know."

"Don't worry, the Fae-rens will take good care of him," Michael piped in.

"We must trust them. I am sure Nicky will be fine. Now let's eat. There is nothing we can do at the moment." Claire stood up, walked over to the cupboard and took out another dish. "Would you like some dinner, Molly?

"I guess I can stay for dinner. I'll call Granny and let her know."

But before Molly could take her cell phone out to call her grandmother, a loud noise erupted. A thundering, almost explosive wind began to blow. All the windows in the Kirkland house began to shake with such fury, that they were at the point of shattering.

Michael Montoya yelled, "Everyone run to the bathroom. It's the safest place."

Then the ground began shaking ferociously. Claire and Molly ran to the bathroom, grabbing the dog on the way. Michael stopped for a moment to snatch up two comforters off the beds. Then he too entered the bathroom and closed the door. "Here, sit down and cover yourself with these," he told them.

But in less than five minutes, the wind stopped and the shaking ceased. The three of them waited for a few minutes to make sure the worst was over before exiting the bathroom. Claire and Michael looked around the house for damage. Molly stood in the kitchen, still in shock from the incident.

Several windows had cracks, but no other serious damage was visible. Then Claire peered out the front door to see part of the roof from Mr. Rosenelli's porch, rested on his neighbor's front yard. There were many broken tree branches lying all over the ground. Mrs. Grey's home seemed untouched, but the rest of the neighborhood looked like a bomb went off. Debris was everywhere.

Claire was still feeling very disturbed by what had just happened and spoke in a quiet voice, "I guess we should try and get back to dinner."

The three of them went back to the kitchen table. They quickly cleaned up the mess on the table from the severe shaking of the house, then sat down and tried to start eating again.

Claire looked over at Michael and declared, "All these tremors and weird weather everyone is having is getting very scary. Tonight it was too close to home. It is very rare to see a tornado in this part of Arizona."

Michael, looking strained, nodded in agreement. Molly was too scared to even speak.

CHAPTER 5

# THE PLAN

In a cave at Black Spirit Butte, Brin-dah was disclosing the plan to Nicky. "Once we give you the Elka and the time is near, the map will help guide you to the copper mine. We will follow you at a distance. Once you enter the mine, you will take out the gold Watch of Wren and hold it in your hand. The gold disk will direct you toward the portal. As you get closer to the portal, the disk will open. Follow the glowing pointer to the entrance of the doorway. As soon as it opens, you must enter. The portal will open for only a half an hour at high sun or your high noon. You must enter behind the veil within that time or you will have to wait for three more days and that would be very dangerous for all. Now, as soon as you step in, there will be a moment when you enter the doorway that you will be suspended in a cloud. You will see and feel nothing. Do not be afraid, for it will disappear quickly. Before you, there will appear a field of tall ferns and many colored flowers as far as the eye can see. Follow the cobblestone path amongst the flowers, until you are met by a white-winged centaur. His name is Kendar. He guards the main entrance to the outer realm. He is aware of your forthcoming. Show him the Watch of Wren and tell him that you seek an audience with the Grand Glymirra regarding the Elka. He will send a telepathic message to Glymirra. It was her plan to enlist your aid and make you a Guardian. She is already awaiting your presence.

"We will need much help from other Protector Fae-rens once you have succeeded in delivering the last Key to Glymirra. The Grand One will need many of the Fae-rens to protect her travel to the grotto, hidden deep in the earth so that she can place all four of the Keys into the triangular Altar of Hope. Then the balance will be set once more and all the terrible occurrences happening to your world will cease and the evil will become much less powerful."

With a puzzled look on his face, Nicky asked, "I don't

understand, Brin-dah. Why is the altar in the Earth instead of in Wren, where it would be more protected?"

"Well, Nicky, in order to heal Gaeya, the Altar must be part of the heart of Gaeya. The Keys of Being will not restore balance if they are anywhere else. That is why our great Glymirra will not reveal the location of the Altar of Hope to anyone. The hidden secret of this site will keep it safe for all time. The Protector Fae-rens must keep the evil ones busy while she uses her powers to unite the Keys of Being once more.

"Tomorrow we will go to the secret cave where we hid the Elka and give it to you. The Grand One said the Key will remember you. It may let you use its powers. Maybe you can become invisible again. It helped you thwart the Cursed One's lackeys the last time."

"For now, you should rest. We shall start our journey as soon as the great sun awakens."

Then without warning, the ground began to tremble. Dust and pieces of the rocky ceiling began to fall. Loud, booming, noises could be heard echoing throughout the caves.

"Oh, no! Hurry! We must take cover."

"Why? Isn't that just the butte's tremors?"

"I no longer think it is just the butte. Before, the tremors were a sign of a former evil presence, but now it must be due to the unstable Gaeya." They all hurried to the shelter of the carved out niche in the cavern wall and waited for the movement to calm.

Der-rex looked at Nicky and said, "Now you see why we must return the Elka as soon as possible."

With a look of anxiety, Nicky nodded to the Fae-ren, as he began to more clearly understand the importance of his mission. It was a little unnerving, realizing that the future of his home and the entire Earth, rested on him returning the Elka to Wren.

Nicky went over to the boulder he sat on earlier, wiped off the fallen dust and pebbles, and then seated himself once more. As he tried to relax, a noise came from the teen's stomach and he realized he was hungry. He opened his backpack and pulled out two sandwiches, one turkey and one peanut butter and jelly. He pulled out a bottle of water and took a sip. *I guess I better save some for tomorrow,* he thought to himself.

"I don't know about you two, but I'm starving." As he began to gobble down the first sandwich, the teen looked up and asked "Hey, do Fae-rens even eat?"

"Yes," Brin-dah responded. "But we eat the fruit that grows in Wren, and we do not need to eat as often as mortals. A Fae-ren can go ten of your days before he or she even feels hunger. But, of course, Der-rex did eat the strange food you gave him when he was transformed into a dog, the first time you met."

Nicky stared at Brin-dah, "Wow, I would be dead in ten days! So how long do you think it will take for me to get the Key to Wren?"

"We hope only one more sun after we retrieve it. The portal is only open at certain times. We must count today as one sun. The longer we wait, the better chance the Cursed One has of finding us. He is becoming more reckless and dangerous. He will do anything to stop Glymirra. It is imperative that when the portal reaches here, you must enter it without hesitation. You will be safe in Wren. Otherwise, you leave yourself open for capture or worse, once you take possession of the Elka."

Nicky stared at Brin-dah, then he swallowed in frightened speculation.

"Where is this...uh...this portal, you know... the door you speak of?" the teen asked in a dry, quivering voice.

Brin-dah explained, "It is not far, about five or six of your miles from the cave where we hid the Elka. I do not know the exact location. As I mentioned, it is in an old mine that has been abandoned for many years. Every three of your days, when the sun is directly above, I believe you call it "high noon", the veil will open with the use of the gold opulan. You will have half an arten of time to enter--in mortal terms one half hour. That is when the portal will align with Wren. You will only have this short time to use the Watch of Wren to open the door and enter into our outer realm. If you miss this time, we must wait three more days. At the present we are unable to travel our usual way using the orb suspended from our necks or riding the warm, swift wind to take you to another portal in another part of Gaeya. The longer it takes you to reach Wren, the more chance the evil Fellon has of discovering our plan and stopping you before you reach Glymirra. Now, we all must rest. Tomorrow we will need all the strength and cunning that we possess to fulfill our destinies."

That night Nicky's sleep was filled with nightmares as he found himself a young boy again, running and hiding from the evil sorcerers and monstrous animals. He tossed and turned even though the Fae-rens had provided him with a kind of mattress made of straw, twigs, and a thick blanket they produced by magic, in hopes of granting him a more comfortable slumber.

Morning came faster than they all anticipated.

Der-rex shook the restless teen awake. "'Tis time we leave."

"I'm not really sure I am ready for this," Nicky sighed as he sat up.

"It will be alright," Brin-dah smiled as she appeared in her human form. "We will go to the cave where the Elka is hidden and remain there until dawn tomorrow. Once the star sun has risen you must use great caution, but also great speed to travel to the copper mine and find the portal. We will give you a magical map, that only you can read and follow. You must reach the doorway of the portal by high sun. Remember the opulan, the Watch of Wren, will guide you once you enter the main chamber of the mine. We will follow you from a distance. Then we will use our magic to divert any evil away from the mine, giving you time to enter Wren. If anything happens, you must protect the Elka and the gold Watch. You must remember that the Key will help you. Use its powers if necessary. If the opulan falls into the Cursed Fellon's hands it may give him a chance to find a portal and enter Wren, destroying all.  For the Veil will never yield to evil. If the Elka falls into his hands, Gaeya and our world as well, will be lost."

Discouraged, Nicky stood up, grabbed his back pack and warily followed the Fae-rens out of the main cave and into the tunnel. The information he was just given made him feel even worse. A huge, huge responsibility weighed on his shoulders. *How can I do this?* he thought.

## CHAPTER 6

# THE DUST DEVIL

The three began to snake their way through the tortuous cavern tunnel. Nicky once again had to walk stooped over to clear the low overhead, but came to an abrupt halt half way through the tunnel. The entire ceiling had collapsed, completely blocking the passage. He realized that he was having difficulty breathing. The air was really thin. Now he was terrified! *How were they to get out?*

Der-rex's light dimmed, and he and Brin-dah turned into humans. They knew that being visible would help calm Nicky. "We will use our magic and remove this obstacle, but it may take a while." Der-rex pointed to a large, flat rock he had moved against the stony wall. "Please, sit down. Do not fret, all will be better soon."

The two returned to their spirit forms, joined hands and began to chant "dissa, dissa , aleev, dissa , dissa, aleev."

The teen was not looking forward to the rest of today, and definitely not to tomorrow, for everything depended on him reaching the portal and returning the Key in a very short time. But that seemed so far away. Now all he wanted was to leave this hazardous tunnel. Nicky sat, watching anxiously as the rocks disappeared, several at a time.

It wasn't long before the tall pile became a small hill. Soon the passage was completely clear. Der-rex turned his light on and Brin-dah helped Nicky rise and continue their journey out of the unstable Butte. In a short time, they had reached the opening of the cave.

Nicky stepped on to the outside ledge and stopped for a brief moment. He was very glad to be out of that cavern. He thought for a time that the Butte could have been his tomb and no one would know he was there. He took in a deep breath and nodded to the Fae-rens that he was ready to move on, knowing more obstacles and dangers were awaiting him.

"Why could you not remove the entire pile at one time?" Nicky asked.

"Because it could have caused another cave-in," Der-rex explained.

"Oh, I guess I thought magic was all powerful."

"No, Nicky. Everything has its limitations, and a cause and effect."

The Fae-rens each took an arm and lowered Nicky to the ground below. He turned and looked back up. He was so glad to be at the bottom of the butte and into the open air. He took a deep breath, closed his eyes and relaxed for a brief moment.

Then without a warning, the Butte and the ground shook worse than ever. A large piece of the rocky overhang, which covered the front of the cave openings, broke off and plummeted down toward them. Nicky yelled, but right as he would have been crushed, he was saved by Der-rex. Looking around, the teen regained his bearings and ran away from the bottom of the mountain toward the dirt road which led to the highway. The ground stopped shaking just as the teen reached the edge of the road. He stopped to regain his footing and breathed another sigh of relief, while searching for the Fae-rens. They appeared in human form in front of him, reassuring and comforting him.

Their next problem was getting transportation to the mountain site where they had hidden the Elka.

"We need to get closer to the main road. There we can catch a ride on the back of a truck, like Der-rex and I did when we traveled to your home."

The three of them moved quickly. It was only a few minutes until they reached the highway ramp. Brin-dah whispered in Nicky's ear, "We will stay in our Fae-ren form to protect you, but we all must jump on the back of that black truck which is approaching. Ready? Now, jump!"

With his long legs, Nicky sprinted and jumped into the bed of an extended cab pick-up truck that had slowed down to enter the highway. He quickly ducked down so that the driver wouldn't see him. As he settled, he judged that they would be heading north.

"How far is it to the place where you hid the Key?" Nicky asked.

"We have about one and a half peri-artens, or one and a half of your hours to ride to the mountain area where the Elka is concealed."

After spending so much time on the move, the ride seemed to take forever for Nicky. He was so unsettled about the pending danger he would have to face. So he tried to think of something else. His mind began wandering to the football stadium and the game he would be missing today. He had divided loyalties. His team needed him, but according to the Fae-rens, the world needed him. That was a monumental responsibility. He wasn't some hero! When he was younger he took everything in stride, but he was older now and a little wiser. He understood fear and danger. They were emotions not to be taken with careless indifference. Death and destruction could be the price he might have to pay.

Nicky was feeling overwhelmed. Just the thought of going to another world and meeting the Caretaker of the Earth was enough to pump fear into his body and make his heart race. But of course, he must evade the evil first, to be able to enter there. Everything he was about to do, seemed so impossible.

Nicky laid down in the bed of the truck, he closed his eyes, and forced himself to think of something other than the immense responsibility that was ahead. He closed his mind and wondered back to school. Soon Nicky found himself on the football field facing the Thunderbird team. Wow, the coach was right these guys are huge, but are they fast.

"Hey Jake, I think we can take them."

"Yeah, you and Jesse should be able to run rings around them," Jake replied as he slapped Nicky on the back. Just then the cheerleaders ran by and Nick waved to Molly as she shook her pom-poms in the air. A large smile came across his face, he was so happy and ready to kick some butt!

Der-rex alerted Nicky with a squeeze of his right shoulder, that it was time to leap from the truck bed. He awoke out of his day-dream and came back to reality with a jerk. The huge smile on his face became an instant frown. The truck was exiting the highway. As it slowed down, he jumped off and the two Fae-rens floated down to meet him. Brin-dah turned into a young woman again. She stood in front of Nicky and once again reassured him that she and Der-rex would be next to him as they made their short journey to the mountain where they hid the Elka.

"But we must stay in our Fae-ren form and take all precautions to prevent the evil from finding us before you have a chance to take the Key to Wren."

Der-rex sent a telepathic message to Brin-dah to let her know he felt a chill of evil presence. Brin-dah did not want to alarm Nicky, so she acknowledged Der-rex's warning and both Fae-rens, unknown to Nicky, began to float closer to him.

Nicky could see the mountain range ahead. It was about a mile away. As he made his way forward, he noticed the huge saguaro cacti. They towered fifteen to twenty feet in the air. He felt so insignificant as he surveyed these giant surroundings. This isolated place seemed untouched by pollution or the expanse of cities. He was truly in the middle of nowhere.

Ahead was nothing but sand, large rocks and cacti as he trekked to the mountains. There were no cell phone towers here. No way to get help. No food or water. He had to put all his trust in Brin-dah and Der-rex. His stomach growled, as it was telling him, he must eat something. All the stress from his mission made him forget the normal things, like food. It seemed so unimportant. But unlike the Fae-rens, he needed food to keep going. Glad he had brought some with him, he reached into the side of his backpack and pulled out a candy bar. He always kept a few extra in his backpack. It was his energy for football practice. He peeled the wrapper and began to eat.

As he marched on closer and closer to the mountains, Nicky's eyes scanned his surroundings for anything unusual. It seemed too quiet, almost eerie. Far off in the distance, he heard the call of a hawk, but beyond that was only the sound of the wind blowing the dusty land around him.

Reading his mind, Brin-dah hovered next to him and whispered in his ear. She wanted him to know that he was not alone. He relaxed a little, but began to walk even faster, hoping to get through this day, even though tomorrow would put him in the deepest of danger.

As they moved closer, Der-rex gently floated down next to Nicky, "'Tis the small mountain to the right." Acknowledging Der-rex with a nod, the boy proceeded to the right.

As the teen advanced, a cold wind suddenly arose around him, swirling the desert sand at tremendous speed and forming a funnel around him. The Fae-rens could do nothing to stop it. They could only look on in horror, as a tall, dark, tornado engulfed him. The sand twisted around and around Nicky with such great speed, it was impossible to move. Wrapped tighter and tighter by the sand, the teen began to felt like an Egyptian mummy. His eyes were closed and his body was totally stiff. He had not expected this. What was going on?

The tremendous pressure pushed so hard on all sides of his body, he could no longer breathe. Nicky knew he was going to die.

Just then, the wind stopped, the dust falling away as quickly as it had come up. Nicky fell to the ground, dazed. He coughed and wheezed, as air filled his starving lungs. Der-rex hurried toward him. Then he reached down and helped pull the teen to his feet.

"What...was...that?" He said, still coughing. "I don't understand. You said they would not know...I was helping you," Nicky said, a horrified look pasted across his face. Brushing himself off and picking up his cap, which had blown several yards away, he turned to the Fae-rens, "I'm not sure I can do this. I don't know if I can be this Guardian.

Why does Glymirra, think I can take on these sorcerers? I have no powers. I'm just an ordinary teenager. Just... an... ordinary human."

Nicky placed his cap on his head, picked up his backpack, shook his head no, and started staggering away from the Fae-rens. Brin-dah grabbed his arm.

"Please, you must stay! You are Gaeya's only hope. I think that binding spell was meant for Der-rex, but you got in the way. They must know we are in the area. After all, the Evil Fellon sent us here when he interrupted our travel route back to Wren. Some of the more powerful sorcerers can still detect our aura no matter what we do. But I think they realized you were not a Fae-ren and released the dark funnel before it could harm you."

Nicky sat on a nearby boulder and tried to collect himself.

Brin-dah turned into a young woman and offered her hand to Nicky. "You must come with us now, before they have time to attack again. You can rest as soon as we reach the spot where we hid the Elka. We have heavy protections there. I sense they have gone for now. We must hurry."

With a very worried look, Der- rex sent a telepathic message to Brin-dah. Let us hope they did not detect the opulan on Nicky. If the evil sorcerers have, they will know he is working with us as a Guardian. This will put him in danger much sooner than we anticipated and will make it more difficult for him to take the Elka to the portal and finally into Wren.

Moving as quickly as possible while holding on to the half-stunned Nicky, they continued their short trek to the nearby mountain range.

"This is the place where we hid the Elka," Brin-dah told Nicky as they faced a small mountain. Nicky looked somewhat dumbfounded. He could see no openings. As if they read his thoughts, the Fae-rens joined hands and minds, chanting softly. To his surprise a narrow entrance appeared in front of them.

Der-rex pushed on the teen's back.

"Please, you must hurry in so we can close the cave opening. It is our only hope of masking our aura. They must not find us or the Key."

The two Fae-rens followed Nicky quickly inside, then

used their powers to reseal the opening of the cave. Nicky felt even more claustrophobic in this tiny cave. The ceiling was so low that the top of his head brushed against it. He quickly looked around for a place to sit. He spied a smooth spot on the floor in the corner of the cavern and sat down with his legs crossed, Indian-style and rested. He was confused and scared at the same time. This idea that he could save anyone, let alone the entire world, was ludicrous...impossible! Where was he going to get the courage to get through this perilous crusade? He felt like running away.

Brin-dah noticed the frightened look on his face and sat down next to him as the mortal young woman. She touched his shoulder to calm him and nodded.

"You will be alright," Brin-dah said smiling. "I know you will not fail us. You were chosen by the Grand Glymirra and have shown great strength and bravery."

Nicky squirmed a little at this uncertainty. Then he looked up into Brin-dah's eyes and responded, "I hope you're right."

Outside the cave, behind a large red rock formation, sat

two of Fellon's sorcerers, their faces hidden in their dark robes.

"We must return to the mountain Fortress and let Shredd know what we found here."

"But, Dreygon, we did not find the Elka, only two Fae-rens with a young human with them. Won't Fellon be angry that we returned without the Key?"

"Tarr, maybe the gold disk the human has is important. We need to return and talk to Shredd."

The two sorcerers transformed into glowing red flames, then disappeared.

CHAPTER 7

# THE FORTRESS

Half a world away, in the tall, dark tower of an old fortress, high in the Himalayan Mountains, a hunched figure shrouded all in black traveled to the top of a steep staircase. He arrived in front of a wide, thick wood and iron door. Sucking in a very deep breath, he reached out his gnarled hand and pulled open the heavy door. It revealed an enormous, cold stone room, lit only by a few torches mounted on the walls. He stepped inside and paused to get his bearings, knowing his message would not be a good one. There in front of him, with his back turned, stood the most powerful, evil sorcerer Gaeya had ever known.

"Cursed One, I need...to speak to you," he said in a deep, wavering voice, as he slowly stepped toward Fellon the

Cursed, with his head bowed. The dark mage was looking at a three-dimensional map, projected in the air before him and created by the blackest magic.

"What is it Shredd?" a harsh, deep voice demanded. "Have they found the Elka in the desert?"

"No."

Fellon whipped around to face Shredd, and with a loud, thunderous voice responded, "Then why are you wasting my time?"

Cowering down even lower, almost touching the stone floor with his nose, Shredd whispered in a shaky tone, "But your Evilness, Dreygon has found the Fae-rens you seek in the desert land in America. They do not have the Elka with them, but they have a young human with them. He did not have the Key, but he had something round and gold on him. Could it be the other object that you have been searching for?"

Shredd kept his head bowed, waiting for the evil Fellon to acknowledge him. No one ever looked directly at the Cursed One. To do so meant instant death.

Fellon's dark, soulless eyes widened and his face

revealed a sinister smile. Then he thought, *I know of no mortal Guardian in that part of Gaeya. Unless Glymirra has appointed a new Guardian. But that does not matter, what matters is this object maybe an opulan. With it in my possession, my evil ones can enter behind the veil and make my threats against Wren a reality.*

"Shredd, take Dreygon and Tarr and proceed to the land where they found this human. Do not return unless you have him and the gold object he has on him. Go, now!"

Shredd bowed once more, turned and scurried out of sight.

Fellon, paused and thought, If the *young human does have the opulan, I can easily take over Wren. I must continue searching for the closest portal. They are not easy to find. I have knowledge that a different one appears in a different part of Gaeya at six or twelve mortal hour intervals, but only Glymirra knows all their locations and times of appearance.*

"According to a Fae-ren that Shredd captured and destroyed, even her most trusted Fae-rens do not know this most sensitive information," he said, talking aloud to himself. "I must have this human and his opulan." Shaking his fist, he shouted, "He has it for a reason, so he must know where a portal exists. I will have it and finally take Wren! Soon, all will tremble at my sight!" His wicked laugh echoed through the tower, as he thought of controlling all.

Fellon had fifteen thousand wicked sorcerers and thousands of bewitched animals like tigers, lions, cougars, panthers, black and brown bears, large dogs and wolves under his control. Many of them were placed in locations all over Gaeya, waiting for orders to take over other more timid animals and, ultimately, the humans.

Fellon had waited more than seventy-five years to get to this point. Now he was closer than ever to taking over, not only Gaeya, but also Wren. No one was going to stop him. He sent a telepathic message to several of his in-house sorcerers to gather in the great hall.

"We must prepare. Soon, all will be mine!"

CHAPTER 8

# SENDING HELP

Back in Wren, using the Reflection of Ages, Glymirra was checking Brin-dah, Der-rex and Nicky's progress. The evil had become so powerful; the mystical crystal could not always detect its presence. But, the Grand One knew the evil would arrive back in the desert after what she had observed. *I must send help without drawing suspicion to the area where Nicky and the portal are located. Nicky must reach Wren with the Elka within the next sun. Otherwise it will give Fellon more time to capture Nicky and obtain the opulan or the Key.*

Glymirra sent for her pterodactyl guard. "I request an audience with the Protector Fae-ren Say-den and her mate Brem-mer. Also bring along one of the Sentinel hawks that returned with Tan-na from Gaeya."

As the pterodactyl left to do the Grand One's bidding, he noticed many of the animals in Wren huddling together, talking and giving frightening glancing to one another. They had lived in Wren for thousands of years, many extinct from Gaeya, in this non-violent world, protected from predators including humans. Even the worker Fae-rens that cared for all the strange animals seemed on edge. Whispering to each other and watching as the pterodactyl walked passed them. *Were they sensing something was not right?* And Glymirra was too busy to council the inhabitants of her Realm at this time. This had never happened before. *What was going on?*

A small worker Fae-ren appeared behind a marble column at the side of the palace entrance. Tan-na was curious to know what was going on, since she knew Brin-dah and Der-rex had not returned with the Elka. After all she had helped the two Protector Fae-rens fool the evil sorcerer on Gaeya. She watched as the pterodactyl shortly returned with the two Protectors and a large, gray hawk, and escorted them into Glymirra's inner sanctum.

"Thank you," Glymirra said as she bowed her head to the guard.

The pterodactyl returned the bow, turned and assumed his post in front of the palace.

The Fae-rens stood at attention, joined by the hawk, awaiting Glymirra's instruction.

The massive half-human, half eagle spread her giant wings and began to speak, " As you are aware, Brin-dah and Der-rex have failed to return with the Elka. They were stopped by the evil Fellon. However, they remain in possession of the Key, but are being hunted on the other side of the Veil by some of Fellon's sorcerers. This makes their return almost impossible. So I have appointed a new Guardian. He was given the gold opulan to open the portal and return the Elka to Wren. I trust him to accomplish this, but he and the Fae-rens with him, will need some help to accomplish this great task."

Focusing on the two Protector Fae-rens, she informed them, "I do not want to bring attention to our new Guardian by sending more than you two to distract Fellon's sorcerers and protect this most important mission. We have less than two suns to achieve our goal. I realize you are not soldiers, but you will have to use your limited powers to trick and fight the evil you encounter. If the evil becomes too overwhelming, you must immediately return to Wren and report back to me. I must know more about Fellon's sorcerers. Brin-dah and

Der-rex must stay to protect the Guardian as best as they can."

Then the Grand One turned to the Sentinel, "As a precaution, I would like you to watch over Nicky's mother and friends. You know the neighborhood. Please do it from a distance, and report any evil you feel or see, at once. This is not going to be an easy task for all of you. But you must do your best to follow my instructions. Both Gaeya and Wren are in danger at this time."

Glymirra, extended her hand and touched the orb suspended from Say-den's neck. "I am sending you to the desert land, in the future, where Brin-dah and Der-rex are hiding. Let them know you have come not only to spy on the evil there, but also to assist them in protecting Nicky, our new Guardian.

"If all goes well, as soon as Nicky reaches the cooper mine, you are to return and report to me regarding the sorcerers' presence. Now, go with great speed."

## CHAPTER 9

# THE SORCERERS
# IN THE DESERT

As the sun rose in the east, Nicky was given the gold opulan, and the Fae-rens prepared him for the dangerous journey to the old copper mine.

"Here is the map you must follow." Brin-dah handed Nicky the strange over-sized, green oak leaf.

"I have never seen a map like this," he said, looking confused, as he reached out his hand and took it from Brin-dah.

"It is controlled by your mind. Just hold it and think of where you want to go, and the directions and landscape will appear. To keep the location of the portal safe, the map will only work for you. Even Der-rex and I do not know it's exact location."

"If you are cornered or think you might be captured, try to hide the opulan and the Key. Also, you may be able to use the magic of the Key to help you. It will remember you.

For you are the only human the Elka has ever acknowledged."

Brin-dah closed her eyes and waved her hand to disenchant the area where the Key was hidden. As it was revealed, she took it in her hand, then handed it to Nicky. He looked at the amber Elka, which began to glow in his hand. He could feel its power and flashed back to the day that it restored his health. He knew it had amazing capabilities, but didn't understand how this small, triangular, amber prism could help control the balance of the entire Earth. It just seemed too small.

"Now wait here while Der-rex and I check for signs of the evil's return."

The two Fae-rens used their powers to open the rocky entrance. Both peered out, then cautiously moved forward, looking over the nearby area as they floated. No cold evil was present. As if conjured up, Brin-dah and Der-rex felt the calming presence of other Fae-rens. Say-den and her mate Brem-mer appeared in front of Brin-dah and Der-rex.

"Glymirra has sent us to assist you in protecting the new Guardian and to spy on any evil that appears here. You must tell us how to elude and fight the sorcerers. We have not faced this evil like you have."

Brin-dah spoke up, "We are glad of your assistance. We must use our cunning and magic to confuse and delay the sorcerers from tracing our new Guardian. Once he leaves the protection of the cave, it will not be long before the evil ones realize the human possesses the Key. The Elka's great energy will make it easier to detect by the more powerful sorcerers, once it is out in the open. Nicky will have only one chance to enter the portal. He must get the Key to Wren. The destruction of the living must stop. He is Gaeya's only hope!

"We must use our orbs to move and transform into animals or even another human. It is the only way to distract them. You will feel the chill of the evil as they arrive, but we must be careful. They have great powers of darkness," She said, as she scanned the desert once more.

"Spread out. Keep a safe distance from the human. We must lead any evil away without totally abandoning him. Der-rex it is time. Please get our new Guardian. He only has a few hours to reach the portal."

Der-rex went back into the cavern to get Nicky. "It seems clear at the moment. Please, you must hurry. We do not have much time."

Nicky stood up in a stooped position due to the low ceiling, grabbed his backpack, and then slipped his cap on. He put the amber Key in his right pocket, while the gold opulan occupied his left pocket. He held the big, leafy map in his right hand and looked around. He hesitated, took in a deep breath in an attempt to relax, which did not work, then proceeded out of the cavern.

The area that lay ahead was a mixture of desert and mountains. Nicky looked down at the strange map he held in his hand. *This is so weird,* he thought. *Where is this copper mine I need to find?* To his surprise, a raised-up path appeared on the leaf-like chart. He needed to walk to the north. *How far is it to the portal?* he asked silently. "5.2 miles" appeared on the map. Thinking out loud as he trekked forward, Nicky said "I should be there in no time if I keep up this pace." He looked up toward the sun. He figured he had a little more than four hours to find the mine's entrance.

The four Fae-rens followed the teen at a distance. But only a few minutes had passed when Brin-dah jumped. The other Fae-rens saw this and then felt the air begin to chill around them.  The sorcerers had returned.

"No, No. We need more time," Brin-dah announced in a frightened voice. "Nicky has not had enough time to even begin his hike to the portal."

"Hurry! We must join forces to protect the Guardian. They must know he has the Elka with him," Der-rex interjected.

The four Fae-rens converged as close to Nicky as they dare, without attracting too much attention to the sorcerers, who were hunting the yet unaware teen. They looked at each other and cringed with fright. How could they know he now holds the Key in such a short time. The Evil here must possess very powerful sorcery. They seemed to be heading toward the boy and the Key.

*Nicky must protect the Elka and we must protect Nicky.* Brin-dah and Der-rex exchanged thoughts. *We must use our powers to distract the sorcerers.*

Brem-mer changed into a desert rat and began to run as fast as he could away from Nicky to try to draw the sorcerers. Then a few yards away Say-den transformed briefly into a coyote and ran the opposite direction from Brem-mer. Brin-dah waved her hand and sent two small dust devil tornadoes towards the evil creatures. They appeared confused.

Der-rex joined in and turned the two small funnels into a small dust storm. The blowing sand made visibility very poor. He sent this telepathic message to the other three "We need to protect our Guardian and his travel to the portal! Help me, keep the dust blowing for a few more minutes."

With everyone's help, the sand storm grew bigger and more intense.

The sorcerers began to get frustrated at their lack of sight, as the gritty sand began to beat against their hooded robes. They put their hands up to shield their faces from the sharp wind.

Angered, the powerful Shredd stood up and a thunderbolt flew out of his finger into the heart of the dust storm. The wind immediately stopped blowing and the dust settled to the ground. "We know you are there Fae-rens. We can see your auras and your goodness. Where is the human? We want the boy."

They began chasing the transformed Far-rens, and firing spells as they advanced. Cacti flew through the air like missiles toward the transformed animals. Brin-dah and Der-rex used rocks and walls of sand as shields against the sorcerers.

Say-den and Brem-mer used their magic to launch large rocks rapidly at the area the where the sorcerers took cover. The sorcerers shot lightning bolts back , causing several of the rocks to explode in mid-air. The Fae-rens changed back into desert creatures, a javelina and coyote, which drew out one of the sorcerers. Brem-mer transformed back into his invisible Fae-ren form, raised his hand and sent a big saguaro cactus spiraling through the air. It grazed Tarr's forehead, as he tried to deflect it with a lightning bolt. They knew they must do everything they could to take their attention away from Nicky. So far, it looked like their plan was working. Nicky was moving away from the conflict and closer to the mine.

Suddenly, the sorcerers stopped fighting the Fae-rens and began moving in the direction Nicky traveled, though he wasn't yet in sight. The Fae-rens kept attacking, but the evil ones continued to pass as if nothing was happening. They seemed focused on another target, the human. Brin-dah and Der-rex exchanged nervous looks. The evil ones must have picked-up on Nicky's trail.

"They know he is close and so is the Elka. We must keep them from reaching Nicky," Der-ex said as he transformed into a teenage boy and tried to lead the evil in the opposite direction.

Would it work? Could he lead the sorcerers away from the Guardian? He hoped they would think he was Nicky.

Out of the corner of his eye, Der-rex saw two sorcerers emerge from behind a tall boulder near him. Their eyes and hands began to glow as they summoned their powers. The Fae-ren closed his eyes, breathed deeply and ran as fast as his temporary human form would allow.

They began to follow behind him. He had succeeded for the time being.

CHAPTER 10

# JOURNEY TO THE COPPER MINE

Moving as quickly and quietly as possible, only stopping for a brief moment to check the direction on the strange leaf map, Nicky continued toward the location of the copper mine. Looking over his shoulder every minute or two to make sure he was alone. His heart was racing... thump, thump...faster and faster it pounded. It was so strong and loud, Nicky feared someone might hear it. He fought to suppress his fear, but to no avail.

There came a strange cracking noise, followed by a sudden chill. Nicky stopped in his tracks. *They're here. I know it. I can even feel them. I guess having the Key in my pocket has given me a sense of forewarning. I have to hide, but where?*

Nicky saw a thick group of acacia shrubs near the foot of a small butte a few yards in front him. He ran to hide behind them, trying to make sure his entire body was hidden. He stooped low behind them, shaking in terror and hoping they had not seen him. But the dark, evil sorcerers were skilled in black magic.

*They will be able to detect me the closer I move toward this butte. I sure hope Brin-dah and Der-rex can help me.*

Unable to see the sorcerers, Nicky felt the chill become colder as they moved nearer. Frost began to form on the ground and nearby cacti as the sorcerers traveled. The dark, cloaked figures seemed unstoppable as they moved closer and closer to Nicky's location. Then something else caught their attention. The teen saw another boy appear out of nowhere, several yards away, close in height and looks to Nicky. *Where did he come from?* Nicky thought.

Shredd motioned for the other two sorcerers to check out the appearance of the strange boy. He knew the Fae-rens could be tricking them. He stayed behind while they investigated.

Nicky relaxed when he saw two dark figures appear from behind a large boulder near him. They turned and started following the strange boy who just seemed to materialize out of nowhere. *Oh, I guess the boy must be Brin-dah or Der-rex,* he said to himself. *Maybe I should leave now. It's getting late.* Feeling scared and alone, he thought, *my time is running out, I must go.*

Nicky did not realize that Shredd was lying in wait for him, concealed behind a very tall, saguaro cactus. Nicky looked around, checked the directions on the leaf map, and slowly stood up, surveying the surrounding area for trouble. Not seeing anything or anyone near him, he decided to continue his journey to the copper min.

Less than 10 seconds after Nicky move out from behind the thick shrubs, a deep chill of air overcame him again. Oh-no! But they were chasing the other boy...how did they find me? Nicky started to panic. He began to jog as quietly as he could, constantly looking over his shoulder. *They must know I have the Elka.*

The hidden Shredd watched Nicky as he came closer and smiled, "I was right! I knew the Fae-rens would try something. I must capture the boy. Fellon will reward me!" Off he went after the frightened Guardian.

Nicky's fright caused him to start running all-out, no longer caring how much noise he made. He had to reach the portal soon.

One of the Fae-rens sent to protect him tried to distract Shredd. Say-den transformed into a coyote and chased after him. Transformed, she knew she would be in a more vulnerable state, but she was no match for the quick Sorcerer. Just as she was lunging in the air toward him, he raised his forefinger and sent a lightning bolt at the coyote. It hit the transformed Fae-ren square in the chest. Her coyote form hung in the air for a second, then dropped hard onto the sandy ground, motionless. Shredd cackled, stepping over her still form, and continued his pursuit of Nicky. Brem-mer, returned to his invisible Fae-ren form, saw his mate fall. Upset, he hid behind a pile of large rocks and waited.

The teen, however, took advantage of the short distraction of Say-den's appearance. He chose a small group of boulders near the foot of a small mountain to conceal himself. He crouched down and tried to catch his breath.

*What can I do? I can't hide the Elka or the Watch of Wren here. They would be too easy to find in this area. I sure hope Brin-dah and Der-rex are close. Hopefully, that coyote wasn't one of them.*

He shivered as he felt a very chill go down his spine. He looked around and to his surprise Shredd was standing next to him. Horror was etched on Nicky's shocked face, as he realized that he had been discovered. He was too overwhelmed to move.

Sadly, he thought, *It's all over.* The Evil would take the Elka and the new Guardian could do nothing about it. Without anyone standing in their way, they could begin their world domination.

The Fae-rens either abandoned him, knowing they didn't have a chance against the dark magic, or else they were destroyed by the other sorcerers. He was all alone. A teenager with no special strengths or powers.

The dark voice washed over him. "Why, hello, boy. I knew it was you! You are older, but I know you are the one who escaped and got away with the Elka five years ago. A mere human tricked me and got away. But never again! In fact, that will not happen today, I assure you. I will send the other sorcerers to your neighborhood to capture your mother and maybe even some of your friends. This way I know you will cooperate with me, until we reach the Fortress."

With a wave of his hand, Shredd bound the teen with an invisible rope and covered his mouth with a thick piece of black cloth. Hearing that his mother and friends were in danger, Nicky began to struggle. "Ummm."

He had to get loose. He had to warn his Mom and save the Elka from Fellon. No one was supposed to get hurt. The Fae-rens had assured him of this. But where are Brin-dah and Der-rex?

Shredd laughed as he watched the teen squirm. His red eyes scanned Nicky's entire body. "I know you have the Elka and the gold disk-like object. I can see them in your pockets. Fellon the Cursed will be pleased that I have brought him both of the objects he was searching for." Shredd was so elated. I know the Cursed One will make me his number one sorcerer and compensate me well for my deeds. "Soon, I will take you to him. He says you have information that he needs to conquer Glymirra and the Fae-rens. Now stay here while I go tell Dreygon and Tarr I have captured the human who carries the Elka and the gold disk."

Grinning, he said to himself, "I will return to the Fortress with the boy, and receive my grand reward."

He looked down at Nicky and sneered. "I will return for you. YOU WILL NOT...make me look like a fool again!"

Shredd began to glow fiery red, then disappeared without a trace. Nicky's eyes widened in shock and fear. He struggled to figure out how he could fight against such powers. Knowing he didn't have any of his own, he knew he still had to try.

CHAPTER 11

# GLYMIRRA'S CHAMBERS

Glymirra went to her chambers, waved a hand over the Reflection of Ages and watched as Nicky and Der-rex departed the cavern. She knew the evil would arrive in the desert soon, even though the magical stone could not always show evil presence. Its darkness often hid from the light of the crystal.

*I must do something. My Fae-rens are no match for Fellon's sorcerers,* she thought. Leaving the Reflection of Ages, she walked to the opposite side of the room, where a large golden egg, twice the size of a brontosaurus egg, sat on a four- foot marble pedestal. The Grand One reached out and touched the top of the egg. Slowly, its sides retracted until all that was left was a book made of gold leaves. She put her hand inside and lifted out the ancient manuscript. It was known as "The Powerous."

Deeply troubled, Glymirra spoke out loud. "In all the hundred thousand years I have kept the balance, I have never once opened this book to receive help. There was never a need for it. The evil is growing too quickly and too many lives are being lost. Until the Keys of Being are united, I must do all I can for Wren. My Protector Fae-rens and even my Sentinels are not fighting soldiers, especially not against the foulest of evil. If they cannot fight back, they could all be destroyed, along with Wren and all of Gaeya!"

The Grand One opened the manuscript to find a language so old and so rare that only she could read and understand it. She fingered the thin, gold leafed, pages carefully, until she found what she was looking for. *This supernatural spell should give my army of Fae-rens and Sentinels powers to protect themselves against the evil and the ability to render the evil ones incapable of injuring anyone or anything.* The spell was a last resort, and using such strong magic was never easy. To keep the balance of the world, what was used by the virtuous could also be used by the wicked in the same way.

As the Grand One contemplated using this potent spell to give her Fae-rens and Sentinels powers equal to the sorcerers hunting them, an alert came in from Gaeya. The grey hawk sent to guard Nicky's family and friends messaged her, telling her that dark sorcerers had appeared near the house on Cactus Flower Lane. He would need more help to protect the humans that lived in the neighborhood.

Immediately Glymirra put THE POWEROUS back, ensuring the massive egg resealed completely. She did not have time to perform the spell. Glymirra had to hurry, so she could dispatch more Sentinels to Nicky's neighborhood. She would only be able to send three, but she would give each one of them a powerful cloaking sphere. These spheres would release an invisible shield around most of the homes and properties to protect the humans from the sorcerers' intrusion.

She summoned her guard. The Grand One would need three hawks to send to Nicky's neighborhood, immediately. In less than one minute the hawks appeared and were given the spheres. With a wave of her large hand, the Sentinels were sent through time to Cactus Flower Lane to join the other hawk protecting Nicky's family and friends. They arrived at their destination in less than five minutes.

Claire, Michael Montoya, and Nicky's girlfriend had just sat down to lunch. The day had been uneventful so far. Everyone seemed a little more calm. Molly, however, was disappointed she had missed cheering in yesterday's game.

Claire stood up and walked over to the kitchen counter to get the salt and pepper shakers. As she reached down to pick up the shakers, she looked out the kitchen window and saw three massive hawks circling close to her house. Their 15-foot wingspans impressive yet ominous at the same time.

"Michael, come here!" she said in a nervous voice. He hurried over to her.

She pointed out the window. "Look. Aren't those the big birds from Wren?'

"I think you are right," Michael agreed. "But why are they here?"

Molly ran over to the window, too. "Oh, this isn't good. I hope Nicky is safe, wherever he is."

Claire stood at the window, shaking with fright, "I

hope he's ok." She hesitated then spoke again, "I'm sure the Fae-rens are taking good care of him. But why are the hawks here? Are they looking for him? Maybe we are in danger. What should we do?"

Michael raised his brow in deep thought, and, looking at both Molly and Claire, he stated, "For starters, I think it would be wise to stay inside and move away from the windows. Molly, I think you should stay here, too. It's the weekend, so no one has to go to work or go to school for a few days."

"But Granny will be worried about me," Molly interjected.

"Molly, we can't take any chances. We need to see what happens in the next few days. What if you are in danger like the last time? We don't know what is happening. I will protect both of you as much as I can. You need to call your grandmother after dinner and let her know you will be staying here for the weekend."

"If there is a problem, I can talk to your grandmother and explain," Claire said.

Calmly, Michael suggested "Now, let's finish eating.

There is nothing we can do at this time. We must have patience."

Lost in their thoughts, the three of them sat back down and ate in total silence. At Claire's feet, Punkin whined softly. She was missing Nicky, too.

CHAPTER 12

# THE ESCAPE

Nicky tried to fight the rope. He began twisting his body left and right, back and forth, but he could not loosen the invisible rope that immobilized him. He moaned and groaned in frustration as he lay on the desert floor near the bottom of a tall, jagged, red rock mountain. Nicky was in a conflicted state. Everything was going wrong. He had failed to make it to the portal. He couldn't hide the Elka or the Watch of Wren. Now his mother and friends were also in danger.

He looked up to see that the sun was moving overhead. In about twenty or thirty minutes, it would be high noon. What could he do to escape? The teen had very little time to make it to the copper mine. He had dropped the leaf map when he was running from Shredd. He had to get loose, find the map, and hurry to the mine.

In his excitement Shredd did not take the Elka or the Watch of Wren from Nicky's pockets. The teen knew he had to find a way to get loose, right now. Then an idea popped into his head and his face brightened up with excitement. A half smiled appeared under the black cloth that covered his mouth. That's it! Brin-dah told him the Key would remember him.

Nicky closed his eyes and concentrated, thinking with all his might, *Release the rope that is holding me and make me invisible.*

The Key in his pocket began to glow. A weird, warm sensation came over Nicky, as he felt the rope fall off around him. Looking down, he saw his feet disappear, then his legs, and finally he could no longer see his hands and arms. He pulled the cloth off from around his mouth and dropped it to the ground.

*Thanks!* he said silently, as he jumped to his feet grabbed his backpack, put on his cap, both which disappeared as they touched his body to begin his journey to the portal. Moving away from the red rock area, he began retracing his steps to look for the leaf map. *Where is it?* He thought. The warm wind picked up. In a few seconds a big, oak leaf flew through the air, landing on the sandy ground at Nicky's feet. Silently thanking the Key for finding the map, he scooped it up in his hand, closed his eyes, and thought, *Where is the mine?* The destination to the mine appeared on the leaf map.

It was very close.

Nicky looked up. The sun was almost directly overhead. He put his hand into the side pouch of his backpack, pulled out an almost empty bottle of water and took a quick swallow, as he moved with great speed toward the mine. It would be noon in three or four minutes. Then he remembered what Brin-dah said, the portal will open for only a half of an hour.

Feeling rushed, but somehow more calm now that he was invisible, Nicky consulted the map once again. He had about a quarter of a mile to go to reach the mine. He broke into a hard sprint and followed the map.

He stopped at an overgrowth of shrubs, which hid the opening to the cooper mine. He pulled and pushed on the bushes, until he had a clear view of an old, boarded up entrance with faded "DANGER" signs posted around it. The timber was so ancient and dry-rotted that it was falling apart.

He noticed two large gaping holes, one on either side.

Nicky tried to crawl through the largest hole, but it was still not large enough to fit through. He pulled his upper body out of the hole. Then he paused for a moment, looking at the boards.  Suddenly, he lifted his right foot, and with all his strength, he kicked one of the rotted slats.  It fell apart with a cloud of dust and splintered wood. The opening was now large enough for the teen to crawl through.

He looked behind him to make sure no one had heard him or followed him, then crawled in.

## CHAPTER 13

# THE COPPER MINE

Nicky stood up on the other side. It was very dark. He started panicking, He didn't have a flashlight or one of the Fae-rens to light his way, and time was running out. He took a few steps forward, but tripped over a pile of rocks and fell. He bounced back up, dusted himself off and stood there contemplating his next move. *What can I do?* Then in the dark, he noticed a slight orange glow coming from his pocket. He reached in the left pocket and pulled out the opulan. It began to vibrate and as he held it, the orange glow brightened a little more. Excitement pulsed through him as the small glow from the Watch of Wren helped his view of the inner cave. He could only see three or four feet in front of him at a time, but at least it was not pitch black. He started to move forward at a faster pace, stepping over broken timber from the shafts above and piles of rocks from the nearby minor earthquakes.

Nicky soon approached an area where the mine pathway divided into three shafts. He came to a halt and thought, *Which way do I go?* He didn't have time to waste, so he began walking quickly to the right shaft, but the opulan's glow dimmed. He passed the middle shaft, but the opulan's light did not change. *Oh! It must be the left shaft.* As Nicky moved toward the far left shaft, the opulan's glow brightened up. As he moved down the left shaft, he spied railroad tracks and an over turned mine cart lying in a pile of copper ore that spilled out of it. He stepped over a few more pieces of timber that had rotted and fallen and several more piles of loose rock. Moving a little faster with excitement at the thought he was very close to the portal entrance, he got careless and fell. Nicky had tripped and his left leg slid under an old railroad tie. His ankle caught underneath it. The teen put the opulan down in the dirt next to him. Nicky would need both hand to pull out his leg from the iron rail. He pulled and pulled, but he was unable to free his lower leg.

He freaked out. Sweat was rolling down his face. What could he do? Time was running out for him to enter the portal. He had to calm down and think. *That's it. Maybe I need some assistance.* Asking out loud, "Please, Key, help me!" Unknown to the teen, a glow came from his pocket. Nicky heard a loud squeaking noise and felt the metal loosen around his ankle. Using both hands, he quickly pulled his leg out, grabbed the opulan, and stood up. Trying to hurry before his thirty minutes was up, he tripped and fell again, almost losing his cap. Lifting himself up once more, he began moving, but this time with more caution.

The teen began to progress further and further into the left shaft. All of a sudden the Watch of Wren, which the teen held in the palm of his hand, started to vibrate faster and with more force, until it opened. Nicky peered inside of the gold opulan to see a thin golden arm with two gold wings attached at the end forming an arrow, which seemed to point toward the wall down the right side of the rocky shaft. He followed it quickly to a strange-looking wall of white sparkling quartz.

When he raised it toward the wall, the gold disk illuminated so radiantly, the teen had to shade his eyes with his other hand. To his great surprise, a dark tear appeared in the middle of the crystal, quartz wall. As Nicky squinted at the dark crack, it began to open wider and grow larger and larger. With a sigh of relief, he knew he had found the portal entrance.

He touched the right pocket of his jeans and felt the prism-like Elka. With all the running and falling, he wanted to make sure that he still had it in his possession, after all, the Key was the reason for his dangerous quest. Nicky was so elated at finally making it to the portal. He took in a deep breath, closed his eyes and stepped forward into the now dark, door-like opening. When the teen opened his eyes, he jerked in alarm to find himself in a giant cloud. He couldn't see anything and somehow he had lost his cap when entering. For a brief moment ,Nicky froze in terror, then he remembered what the Fae-rens said. The cloud would disappear and he would find himself in a field of large ferns and very tall, yellow flowers. He was to follow the stone path to the white-winged centaur, who guarded the entrance into outer Wren.

Smiling, he moved forward confidently. He had made it into Wren! He had completed his dangerous task. No more evil sorcerers to chase him or evil enchanted animals to corner him like last time. No evil would chase him ever again. The only challenge remaining was meeting the ominous Keeper of the Balance, the Grand Glymirra.

The cloud soon lifted and Nicky could see large green ferns blowing in the warm breeze, with a cobblestone path ahead, lined by fields of ten or twelve feet tall, yellow, sunflower-like plants. As he began walking down the path to locate the white–winged centaur, a sense of euphoria and serenity rolled over him. The fear of meeting the Grand Glyimirra had left him. Continuing to follow the path forward, the teen slowed down to take in all the beauty and enjoy the feeling of total peace within himself. He could smell the light flowery aroma which filled the air around him. As Nicky progressed down the path, he saw fields of flowers representing  almost every color, spread out ahead of him. In the distance, the teen spied a rainbow with the most vivid colors he had ever seen. It looked as if it was solid and maybe if he was closer he could touch it. Nobody could appreciate the sights before him.

As a human, he would not be able to see the best part of Wren. According to the Fae-rens no human had ever seen the inner realm. Violence had never touched the peaceful kingdom. Nicky could only imagine how wonderful it must be to know only peace and to see animals thrive that were now extinct on Earth. He wandered would it would be like to see a dinosaur or a dragon. Maybe there were animals like unicorns once on Earth.

He moved at a steady walk toward his destination. Soon Nicky reached Kendar, the centaur. His eyes widened and his mouth opened as he approached the creature. He had never seen such a marvelous sight. To his knowledge, no human had. Centaurs were things of legend and myth. How special the teen now felt!

With a large staff in his right hand, the tall, stately, white-winged centaur waited for Nicky to stand directly in front of him. His penetrating green eyes, seemed to take in every inch of the teen. His deep, growling voice said, "You...are the new Guardian? You have the Elka and the opulan with you? "

Nicky bowed his head yes as an answer to each question.

"If all is true, show me the opulan as identification. "

Nicky looked down and realized the gold disk was no longer in his hand. His face went pale with fear. He did not remember dropping it. After all, he was able to enter the portal. Nicky put his hand in his pocket, but the gold Watch of Wren was gone. He searched frantically throughout his jacket pockets and jeans but came up empty.

Panicked and terror-stricken, he announced, "Oh, no! I must have lost it when I entered the portal. I must go back down the path to look for it."

"No!" the centaur boomed. "You must remain here." He pointed his staff at Nicky. "I must consult with the Grand Glymirra. She will know if you are the true Guardian. You must give her the Elka as soon as she arrives. She may be able to use her powers to locate the opulan."

Kendar put his finger to his forehead, and closed his eyes as he sent a telepathic message to Glymirra.

While Nicky waited to meet the Grand Glymirra, the sorcerer, Shredd, met up with Dreygon and Tarr. The pair had stunned two of the Fae-rens as they transformed into various animals and a human, trying to distract them from following the boy.

Brem-mer, who saw his mate struck down by Shredd, had hid behind some rocks, listening and waiting. While the sorcerers talked, the Fae-ren was able to sneak past them. Quietly, he pulled the lifeless Say-den to safety behind the large rocks.

Shredd cackled and rubbed his hands together. "I have captured the human. He is the same boy who had the Elka before. Tie up these Fae-rens, then put them in the cover cage. We may have use for them later. But for now I want you both to go to Cactus Flower Lane and capture the boy's mother in case we have any problems returning him to the Fortress. I know once we are there, he will not be able to resist the Cursed One. Soon the human will disclose all the information needed to conquer Wren and take over Gaeya."

Brem-mer hearing this, knew he must report to Glymirra and get help for Say-den. Using the few seconds of distraction, he touched his orb as he held on to his transformed mate, and the two spirit creatures traveled with great speed to Wren.

Shredd had a huge grin across his face as he began

glowing fire red, "Now I will take the human to the Cursed One and be rewarded." Then he disappeared.

Tarr and Dreygon, quickly tied up the spirit creatures who had transformed into a desert animal called a javelina and a teen boy, who resembled the teen. The two were then placed into an invisible cage. They would take Brin-dah and Der-rex to the Fortress, as soon as they captured Nicky's mother.

Reappearing in a matter of seconds, Shredd returned to the spot behind the bushes where he left Nicky bound. But to his surprise all he found was the black cloth that covered the teen's mouth and the ropes that bound his legs and arms, lying on the ground. He bent down, picked up the cloth and scowled, "How...How did he get away?" He screamed, "No, No, not again!"

He began to jump up and down in frustration. "How... how could a mere... mortal boy... get away. There was no one here to help him. I must find him, before Fellon realizes I let him escape. He must not get the Key to Glymirra. Fellon will destroy me, if that happens. I must...I must find him soon," Shredd said in desperation, as his whole, dark body shook with terror. "No one must know that he got away. I will call upon all my powers to locate him. I must find him before he gives the Elka to someone to take to Glymirra."

Shredd tried and tried to find the trail Nicky left, but his magic was not strong enough. After fifteen minutes of summoning and casting spells, he was unable to locate the direction in which Nicky had gone. Finally, he decided he must rely on Tarr and Dreygon to aid him. Time was running short. Fellon would be expecting him to return with the boy in a day or two. After all, three sorcerers should be able to corner a human who possessed no powers, in a very short time time. He sent a telepathic message to the other two sorcerers to meet him back where they left the caged up Fae-rens. Then his dark image became flaming red and he vanished into thin air.

# MEETING THE GRAND ONE

Nicky waited to meet Glymirra. He was beginning to get nervous again. Yet he could also feel a strange, peaceful calm soak through his body. He thought, *I am so lucky. Look at this amazing place. No one would believe me if I told them of the beauty I see here, or that I was greeted by a mythical centaur or that I, a mere human, is going to meet the Care Taker of the whole World.* Reaching Wren, made all the danger Nicky went through seem so minimal now. Nothing, nor no one could understand what he was seeing and what he was feeling. Elation filled his entire body. "I am the Guardian! I did It!"

Then Nicky's exhilaration ceased as he remembered the threat Shredd made. He was sending his sorcerers to abduct his Mom and maybe his friends. Once again he had mixed feelings, one of accomplishment and the other of terror for those at Cactus Flower Lane. He felt helpless. Maybe he could ask Glymirra to send him home. Someone had to alert them of the impending danger. He fidgeted as he thought of the danger, and waited in silence with Kendar.

Glymirra was in her chambers consulting the Reflection of Ages, the very large flat, blue crystal which hung on the far wall. She saw as the three Sentinels arrived at Cactus Flower Lane. They flew over the gray hawk that was waiting for them. All of a sudden the three new hawks ascended one hundred feet above the houses and dropped the magical golden eggs they held in their talons, given to them by Glymirra. In less than two seconds, an invisible shield covered over half of the Kirkland's neighborhood, with Nicky's house at its center. As long as everyone stayed within that area, they would be protected from the evil.

Just then she received two telepathic messages. The first one was good news from Kendar announcing the arrival of Nicky. The second was from the Sentinels letting her know that many dark creatures had just appeared in Nicky's neighborhood.

The Grand One sent back a message to all the Sentinels, "Stay hidden.

Attack only if you feel it will deter the evil. The shield will hold-up even to the strongest sorcerer. Only Fellon himself may be able to cross it. But I think he has more important problems right now. As a precaution, I will send Tan-na in a human form to explain to Nicky's mother that she and her neighbors need to remain in their dwellings for the next few days. They will be protected there."

Once again Glymirra summoned her pterodactyl guard. He appeared immediately in front of her and bowed deeply with his winged arm, crossing his chest.

"Please bring Tan-na to me."

He left and soon returned with the worker Fae-ren.

Tan-na was feeling a little uncomfortable. Why would the Grand One need to see her? Maybe, she was to be punished for following Brin-dah to Gaeya.

Reading her mind, Glymirra stated ,"No, Tan-na, you are not being disciplined. I need your help," she stated while calming her with a wave of her hand.

Tan-na looked up with surprise and relief in her face, then bowed again. Then she asked, "Me? How may I assist you Grand One?"

"There is a problem on Gaeya. You were at the Kirkland's home with Brin-dah and Der-rex. You know the area. The Evil Fellon has sent a few of his stronger sorcerers to bewitch or capture Nicky's mother and friends. I have sent a great protection over them, as long as they stay within their dwelling. The protection only extends so far.

"I will transform you into a young woman and send you there. You must explain to Nicky's mother that he is safe, but that his family and friends are in grave danger if they leave my protection.

"Nicky has brought me the Elka. Soon I will travel to the Altar of Hope and place the four Keys where they belong. Gaeya's balance will be returned, and Fellon and his followers will lose much of their power. Then we can help Gaeya to regain her balance.

"Now, come closer. I must make you human."

With a wave of the Grand One's hand, Tan-na was no longer a spirit, but a thin, young woman with long brown hair, a blue tee shirt and jeans. Tan-na looked down at herself and smiled.  It was such an honor to be given this important job.

"Remember Tan-na, you do not have powers on Gaeya like a Protector Fae-ren.  Once you have let everyone know what is happening, you must return here immediately. Do you understand?"

"Yes, Grand One. I will do as you ask."  Tan-na answered in a quiet voice.

"Here is your orb. It will take you to Gaeya and back."

Tan-na put the orb around her neck. Glymirra gently touched it, and Tan-na disappeared, traveling on the wind through space and time to the Kirkland's home.

Glymirra felt pleased that all was going well. Spreading her massive wings, she flew out of the palace sanctuary and to the outer perimeter of Wren to meet with Nicky.

## CHAPTER 15

# CACTUS FLOWER LANE

Michael Montoya tried to ease Claire's and Molly's minds, although he too, was worried about Nicky. No one there knew where the teen was, or how to get in touch with him. The three of them were trying to recover from the twister. They sat at the kitchen table, discussing the presence of the hawks in their neighborhood, when someone knocked on the door. They all looked at one another in question. Who could it be? Punkin ran to the door barking.

Michael stood up. "I'll get it."

He walked over and opened the door. Tan-na stood at the door in her human form.

The police officer looked puzzled and asked, "Can I help you?"

The young woman smiled, "I am called Tan-na. I have come from the world of Wren. The Grand Glymirra has sent me to explain what is happening at this time. I have an important message for you."

"It's nice to meet you. I am Michael, a friend of Nicky's. Please, come inside," Michael offered, as he opened the door further.

"Thank you for your invitation. As a Fae-ren I cannot enter your dwelling without turning to stone. I will stay here at the door to give you this message. Then I must return to Wren."

Hearing this, Molly and Mrs. Kirkland stood up and moved closer to the open door to listen to the message.

"First, know that Nicky is safe, but unable to return to you at this time."

Mrs. Kirkland and Molly felt relieved at this news, and hugged each other tightly. They waited to hear the entire message.

"Soon, Gaeya, your Earth, will heal and all will return to normal in a few of your weeks. But the powerful evil has come to this Cactus Flower Lane, so the Grand One has sent four Hawks, our Sentinels, to protect you. She has also covered a large area with a powerful shield, but it is not large enough to cover everything in this neighborhood. It is imperative that you stay within the invisible protection provided. The hawks are positioned at each end of the shield's boundary. As long as you remain inside the perimeter, no evil can harm you. Now I must leave you. Please stay safe."

Tan-na touched the orb that hung around her neck and winked out of view, traveling swiftly back to Wren.

Unknown to the inhabitants of Cactus Flower Lane, Dreygon and Tarr had arrived at the other end of the neighborhood a little while earlier, sent there by Shredd. They hid inside a storage shed, where they began planning how to use their black magic to secure Nicky's family and friends. They wanted to use them as possible bait to coerce Nicky into revealing information, which might help Fellon and his dark sorcerers take over Wren.

But as they advanced closed to the Kirkland house, they were met with resistance from the invisible shield cast by the Sentinels. They shot thunderbolts at the shield, but the bolts deflected by the shield flew back, narrowly missing the sorcerers as they exploded in the air. They decided to recite a removal spell together in order to eliminate the protection. They tried again to infiltrate the Kirkland's yard, but the sorcerers were thrown to their backs several feet away.

Retreating from the entrance of the Cactus Flower Lane, the two evil ones stood in confusion and conferred. Tarr looked at Dreygon.

"What magic is this? The Fae-rens have no such awareness of powerful force fields. Where did it come from?"

While standing there, to their surprise, the hawks attacked the two sorcerers. The sounds of large, flapping wings, beating down on them, and terrible high-pitched screeching could be heard a block away. The hawks pecked and their sharp talons ripped the cloaks and gowns of Tarr and Dreygon.

The sorcerers were quickly overpowered by the Sentinels. They cowered down to protect themselves, wrapping their arms around their bloody heads and torn clothing. The attack had been fast and furious, leaving no time to fight back.

"We must get...out...of...here, now! We must...tell Shredd." Dreygon's frightened voice said. Tarr agreed.

Both sorcerers turned a fiery red and disappeared.

They returned to the northern mountain area, where Shredd was awaiting their appearance.

The Sentinels returned to their posts. A telepathic message was sent to the Grand One, letting her know they had sent away the evil. They won this battle, but how many more would they face?

CHAPTER 16

# THE ELKA'S RETURN

Glymirra landed a few feet from Kendar and Nicky. Kendar bowed to the Grand One. Nicky was in total awe at the sight of the majestic ruler. His jaw dropped for a moment, as he stared at the very tall, half white eagle, half human-looking Keeper of the Balance. Wow, he never expected the Keeper of the Balance to look like this. As the teen kept staring in almost a trance-like state, Kendar looked over at Nicky and then pointed his staff at the ground. Nicky jumped at the motion. He sucked in a breath, realizing he was being disrespectful. He immediately dropped to one knee in front of her.

Her large, round, piercing, blue eyes seemed to look right through him. The silence seemed to grow, and Nicky began to get very nervous once more. But the Grand One eased his mind.

Using a soft, serene tone, she began to talk. "Please rise. Nicky, I knew you would not let either of our worlds down. Thank you for all your help. I know the mission I entrusted you with was very, very perilous. If our worlds did not need you so much, I would never have put you in such danger. As a new Guardian, you did not get the chance for much training and guidance before having to undertake this task. You did an admirable job. Unfortunately, we do not have a lot of time. Now, I need you to give me the Key."

Nicky reached into his pocket and pulled out the amber Elka. He held it in his palm, marveling that such a small, innocent-looking stone could be so powerful and create so much trouble. He slowly handed it over to Glymirra. She took it and slipped it behind some feathers around her waist.

"Kendar told me that you no longer have the gold opulan with you. I consulted the Reflection of Ages. It showed you dropping it inside the mine just as you entered the portal. I will send someone to retrieve it. The evil must not find it, otherwise Fellon and his sorcerers may be able to enter our peaceful realm.

"I must also tell you. I sent four Sentinels to your neighborhood to protect your mother and your friends. I do not want to worry you, but I feel it is important for us to be careful and take precautions. The growing evil is becoming desperate."

Still awestruck by her presence, Nicky shook his head to clear his thoughts. He had momentarily forgotten what Shredd told him regarding kidnapping his Mom. He didn't think his involvement with the Fae-rens would affect his Mom or anyone else. Anxiety filled his mind and his stomach felt like it was tied in knots. Nicky could keep quiet no longer and spouted out, "Please! I must go home now. I have to help them! Can you send me back?"

Glymirra smiled gently at the human. "I know you are afraid for them. Do not be. For I have sent not only the Sentinels, but a powerful, invisible shield to keep out the evil. No one can harm them. I will send you home as soon as I return the Keys of Being to their proper place in Gaeya. It is imperative the balance be set as soon as possible. It will weaken the darkness growing over Gaeya. She is in danger of collapsing. Your world as you know it could end unless we can reset the balance. That is why your mission was so important."

This news was shocking to Nicky. He knew something wasn't right with all the crazy natural disasters that seemed to be getting worse, but he had no idea it was this bad. The teen began to pace. Then he put his hands over his head. There was nothing ...nothing he could do. Glymirra walked over to Nicky, reached out her large hand and touched the top of his head to calm him down.

"Do not worry. Since I have all four Keys of Being, I can now return them to the grotto and place the them in the Altar. Gaeya will begin to heal. The healing will be quick and the chaos on Gaeya will abate. The sinister power that has a hold on Gaeya will lessen fast and dramatically.

"You must stay and rest here until I have returned. Kendar will bring you some food and drink. I will be back within two of your suns. You will then be sent back to your home on the day Brin-dah and Der-rex first enlisted your help. All will be as it was."

CHAPTER 17

# THE HUNT

Shredd was so upset with himself that he was happy to see Tarr and Dreygon, who had just appeared in front of him. Tarr immediately told Shredd of the problems they faced at Cactus Flower Lane.

"The hawks have become more powerful. The boy's family and friends are well protected. We could not penetrate the invisible barrier which surrounds them. But we still have two Fae-rens tied up that we can take back to the Cursed One, and you still have the human. He will make them talk."

Shredd hesitated. He did not know what to say. He had lost Nicky and the other two sorcerers could not capture his mother for leverage. He knew the mighty Fellon would strike them down with a mere lift of his finger, if he found out they all had failed, once again.

Dreygon studied the look on Shredd's face. "We failed our mission but you still have the human boy and the Key. That is what the Cursed One wants. The boy will not be able to resist the evil of Fellon. He will tell him anything he needs to know."

Shredd suddenly blurted out, "The young human has escaped! If he is able to get the Elka to Wren, Glymirra will be able to stop us by uniting all the Keys of Being. There is no doubt if that happens, Fellon will destroy us! We must find him. He has both the gold disk and the Key."

"I don't understand. You left him here...with the Key and the gold object?" Tarr asked puzzled.

"Yes, and I greatly underestimated the boy. He must have received help from some other Fae-rens. He could not have escaped by himself. Now we must use all our dark powers to locate him and the objects he possesses. If we pull our powers together, I know we can find him."

Afraid of Fellon's wrath, the three of them joined hands and sent out a tracking spell. In no time, the sorcerers had located Nicky's trail. They traveled through the north desert to the location of the copper mine entrance, where the portal had been hidden.

"Curious. The boy's trail goes in but does not come out. He must be hiding in there." Shredd announced, as he pushed backed the shrubs that covered the opening.

He showed Tarr and Dreygon the spot in the old boarded-up entrance that had been broken by Nicky. The three sorcerers crawled through the tight, jagged opening. Once they were through, Shredd used his magic to light up the mine tunnel.

The trio proceeded slowly forward, following the magic that lit Nicky's path until they reached the fork that opened up into three separate shafts. Without warning, the entire tunnel began to shake violently. Rotted pieces of wood that had once supported the ceiling and walls of the mine began showering down on them, mixed with loose rock. They used their dark powers to put a protective armor around themselves, while they looked for a place of safety. The rubble bounced off the shield and fell around them.

Not readily finding a secure location in the trembling tunnel, they turned flaming red, disappeared and then reappeared at the outside entrance of the mine. All around them the ground still quaked.

As the three sorcerers waited for everything to stop shaking, Shredd informed the other two, "We have to go back in as soon as this strong tremor calms. The boy must still be in there. After all, it has been less than thirty minutes since I held him. He had a reason for entering this mine. We must find out why."

Tarr and Dreygon exchanged a look at this demand. They were glad they had powers to protect themselves from the chaos caused by the global unbalance but remained uncomfortable at the idea of proceeding with the hunt for Nicky and the Elka.

It took several more minutes before the earth stopped rumbling. Dust spewed out from the mine entrance, covering their already dusty robes.

"We have no choice but to continue searching the mine. The boy has to be trapped in there. Remember he has no supernatural powers. He cannot move like we can." Shredd declared.

Dreygon and Tarr sighed, but not wanting to face Fellon's wrath, they decided to follow Shredd.

The dark sorcerers moved deeper into the entrance

of the cave. Shredd stepped inside to assess the damage. He waved an arm, and Tarr and Dreygon joined him. Once again he lit the way, and they moved forward. There were extreme amounts of debris covering the floor of the mine. It was almost impossible to step through it, so Shredd decided to use magic. With a wave of his hand, three hover boards appeared. The sorcerers hopped on them and began moving quickly through the mineshaft, ducking often to avoid the broken supports hanging from the ceiling. Soon they reached the area where the mine divided into the three shafts.

"Which way do we go, Shredd?" Tarr asked.

Shredd hesitated for a minute, looking for the faint trail revealed by his magic. It seemed to end here, rather than going into any of the shaft. Resignation overcame him.

"I don't understand. I don't know. We may have lost the trail. It looks like it ends here."

Dreygon and Tarr started to swear furiously. "What do you mean, you don't know?"

Lifting his hand to them, Shredd yelled, "Wait! Let me think."

Shredd stepped off his hover board. Sweat appeared on

his brow. He began to pace in the small spot left untouched by the tremors. He stopped, raised his hands and began to chant.

After several minutes, he quieted, as his hands fell to his sides in despair. His magic was of no help. He simply could not find the trail. *I am doomed. We are all doomed.* He was petrified by this thought. No one failed Fellon and lived.

"I cannot fail! You two, come here," he growled.

Tarr and Dreygon leapt off their hover boards and approached Shredd, their arms crossed and their expressions showing their anger.

"We need to combine all of our magic again. My magic is not strong enough by itself. If that doesn't work, we will separate and search each shaft until we find the boy or some sign of the him. Now, let us begin." They stood in a circle and joined hands. The three of them cast a tracking spell again and again.

"It's not working!" Shredd screamed in frustration. "The earthquake must have covered all trace of his trail. We will have to search all three shafts, until we find the boy and why he came here."

Shredd pointed to Tarr, "You take the right shaft.

Dreygon will investigate the center shaft, and I'll take the left one. We have to locate the boy soon. If you find him, message us. The Cursed One will destroy all of us if he finds out we lost him."

"But Shredd, we did not lose the boy," Tarr smirked. "You did. You alone will incur Fellon's wrath."

"Don't be stupid, Tarr. Fellon will blame all of us." Shredd interjected.

Dreygon, looking terrified, nodded his head in agreement. He knew Fellon's temper all too well.

"Now, quit wasting time! Let's move forward."

The three dark sorcerers separated and began their searches of the mine shafts. Because of the cave-ins, they would have to use their dark powers to clear a path through the debris to advance into the shafts. The search would take time.

CHAPTER 18

# GLYMIRRA'S JOURNEY

Back in Wren, Glymirra left Nicky with Kendar at the outer perimeter of the realm and return to her palace sanctuary to prepare for her journey to the Altar of Hope in the far depths below the Earth's crust. She knew the evil was growing faster than ever, and the conditions on Gaeya were getting out of hand. She needed to hurry as fast as she could to reach the opening of the Grotto. If Gaeya's surface turned to severe ruin, even the Keys may not be able to correct the balance. Extinction of many species may very well be imminent.

Once ready, the Grand One would use some of the Protector Fae-rens to cover her trip to the Grotto, where the triangular, quartz crystal altar resided. She wanted to reach it without any confrontations from Fellon or any of his sorcerers.

Glymirra entered her chambers and hurried over to a large, oak box, sealed with her gold-wings emblem. It sat on a marble table, beneath the Reflection of Ages. The Grand One moved her left hand over the box, and it opened. Inside the now glowing box were three of the four Keys Of Being, the Torka, the Pera, and the Gara. Representing the winds, the seas, and fire. She took them in her hand and placed them in a small red pouch that hung around her wide waist. Reaching her hand behind some side feathers, she pulled out the Elka, the Key of Healing and Rebirth that she received from Nicky. She placed this Key into the pouch with the others.

To prevent losing any of the Keys as she traveled, she chanted a spell and moved her hand in a circular motion around the pouch. They were now secure. She placed a blue cloak over her shoulders and exited her chambers.

As she moved to the entrance of her sanctuary, the grand leader was stopped by the Protector Fae-ren, Brem-mer, looking travel worn and bruised. He was holding his lifeless mate, Say-den. In his distress, he made a small bow and sucked in his breath, as he whispered, "Can you help her?" Glymirra raised her hand and moved it from head to tail of the coyote, checking for any sign of life. Without a word Glymirra shook her head no. "I am so sorry, Brem-mer. Her aura was extinguished by a very powerful sorcerer. You know how vulnerable a Fae-ren becomes in another form. She was very brave to sacrifice herself so that the Guardian could bring me the Elka. She died very honorably."

"But...I understand Der-rex was revived while he was transformed. Can you not do the same?"

"Yes, but he was injured by being thrown up against a wall, not by a powerful thunderbolt hitting the center of his essence. He still had the breath of life within him. I am sad to say that Say-den does not.

"I have lost several of my Fae-rens. I feel the loss of each one, every time a Fae-ren's aura is snuffed out. Ever since my most powerful Fae-ren , your leader Phan-non, was destroyed, I have felt their essence leave us. Very soon, my Protector Fae-rens will suffer no more. They only need to fight the strong evil a little longer. For once the Keys are in place, the balance will lessen all sorcerers' powers. Their control over Gaeya will become less, and the balance will begin to restore in Wren as well."

But Brem-mer hung his head in despair. He barely heard anything Glymirra said. What was he going to do without his mate? They had been together for thousands of years.

Glymirra moved closer to Brem-mer. She touched his shoulder. He looked up with tears in his eyes.

Then the Grand One spoke in a whisper, "I know you have suffered a great loss. But I must ask you, do you have any important information that could help us defeat the sorcerers?"

Brem-mer pushed his grief aside, as he thought.

"At first, we only knew of two sorcerers. We were able to keep them away from the Guardian until a third, more powerful one jumped out from behind a large cactus. He somehow deflected all our magic. He is the one who tried to follow the boy, but then Say-den attacked and was struck down. Der-rex and Brin-dah were stunned by other sorcerers and were paralyzed. Grand One, I must tell. In my desire to save my mate, I almost forgot. Brin-dah and Der-rex are prisoners of the sorcerers! They are planning to take them to a place called the Fortress.

"I was able to pull Say-den's coyote form behind

some large boulders and hide as the evil ones talked. The more powerful sorcerer left but returned an instant later. Just before touching my orb to travel here, I heard him say he would need the help of the others to combine their dark magic in order to find the boy's trail."

Brem-mer sighed and continued, "At least I know the loss of my mate was not in vain, since her direct attack on the sorcerer helped the Guardian return the Elka to you. I thought the more powerful sorcerer had captured the boy, but you tell me he entered here safely and with the Key."

Glymirra reassured him. "Yes, the Guardian was held for a short time by the evil one, but was able to escape and enter the portal to Wren. Now, I am on my way to the Grotto, to return the Keys of Being to their proper place in the Altar of Hope. Time is of the essence."

"Now, take care of Say-den's burial and begin your mourning."

Brem-mer left Glymirra side, leaving her to continue her preparation.

CHAPTER 19

# SEARCHING THE MINE

Tarr, Dreygon, and Shredd each entered their designated shafts. Tarr took the right shaft, Dreygon the center shaft and Shredd entered the left one. The debris from the earthquake was everywhere. The shafts were so narrow and more treacherous since this last severe tremor. Large chunks of rocky wall and broken pieces of timber lay in piles all over the floor of the mine. Sharp pieces of timber used to hold up the ceiling hung like stalactites, ready to pierce the careless. They each had to move with extreme caution, and use their magic to clear the paths as they began searching for any sign of Nicky.

Everything inside the mine was unstable. New cave-ins were just a matter of time.

Tarr and Dreygon were not as powerful as Shredd. Therefore, they moved very slowly and expended a lot more magic, causing them to tire easily and take many small breaks. Fear of being buried alive made them both hesitate every time they heard even the smallest noise.

Suddenly, it sounded like a speeding train was roaring through the tunnel and dust began to fill the cavern. An aftershock had hit the area. Tarr watched in horror as the walls on either side of him begin to collapse in on themselves. He was so afraid of being trapped without hope of being rescued, he decided to run. His body turned fiery red disappearing out of the shaft in an instant and then reappearing outside of the mine.

He would not risk his life for Shredd. After all, he was not the one who had lost the Key and the boy. As much as he feared Fellon, he would take his chances back at the Fortress. As he began to walk away, he had second thoughts about leaving. He dreaded being punished...or even worse. So for now, he would wait outside for a few moments to see if the other two sorcerers were successful.

Dreygon did not like the idea of walking through an unsafe mine shaft waiting to be crushed or trapped, but he was afraid of Shredd and even more terrified of the Cursed One. He was slowly descending the debris around him into the middle of the center shaft when he heard and felt the aftershock. He froze for a moment, listening for movement and trying to determine where the tremors were coming from.

As he was looking around, a slight sound from the ceiling caught his attention. He glanced up and a second later, the rocky ceiling above him cracked with a loud rumble. Large chunks of rock showered down on his head and shoulders, though he tried to cover his head. He was buried alive in a few seconds, only one of his hands visible, reaching up out of the rock. It moved weakly a few times. Then stopped. After a minute or two, the hand turned black and shriveled up. Dreygon was no more.

Shredd followed the left shaft. Using dark magic, he formed a shield around himself. He would not let any of the falling rock or timber touch his evil body. He heard the loud roar and felt the intense rumbling of the aftershock. He stopped moving, waiting for the shaking to cease.

The walls and ceiling had caved-in just behind him. The mortal boy could not have survived that, he thought gleefully. He put his hand out in front of him, levitating and then disintegrating large piles of rocks and debris that obstructed his path as he moved further and further down the shaft.

He wandered if the other two sorcerers had found any sign of Nicky yet. He sent them a telepathic message, asking their progress.

Tarr hesitated a moment before answering Shredd. *No sign of the boy in this shaft.*

Shredd nodded to himself. As he continued forward, he waited and waited for Dreygon's response, but it did not come. He did not know what to think, but he must continue his search. *The boy had no powers, so he must be trapped here!*

This far into the cave, Shredd decided to try a tracking spell again. He became excited, as the magic showed a faint trail of the boy's essence. At last he may have picked-up on Nicky's trail. So he progressed toward what remained of the right side wall in the left shaft. It showed another opening within the cavern.

Shredd proceeded through.

Chunks of colorful quartz crystals lay scattered everywhere, as if a bomb had gone off. He moved a little slower through this area, scanning everywhere for signs of the human.

Using his magic, the sorcerer raised his hand and lifted up massive pieces of rock and crystal, searching underneath them for any sign of the boy. After ten minutes of this, he became frustrated that he had not found any sign of the human.

Once again the dark mage summoned a tracking spell. This time the results were definite. Nicky was here. Shredd summoned the other two sorcerers to help him find the boy.

When Tarr received the telepathic message from Shredd, he cringed and stalled. He did not want to re-enter the mine under any circumstance. He was not sure what he was going to do.

Meanwhile, Shredd kept searching the area where the quartz crystal wall had partially shattered. He thought he saw a piece of clothing under a thick pile of crystal debris. He used his forefinger and pointed it at the crystal debris to move it. Then he noticed something blue sticking out from beneath a large rock crystal. He bent down and pulled the object out from the debris. It was a boy's baseball cap-- the same one Nicky had on when Shredd captured him earlier.

A huge, sinister grin spread across the sorcerer's face. Searching for the body of the boy to confirm his demise, he noticed something shiny sticking out of the pile next to where he found the hat. Elated, he dug swiftly with his hands to recover the entire object. As he pulled it out, he noticed it was one of the objects the boy was carrying.

He held it up in his right hand, while snapping his left hand to create a flame so he could look more closely. It was a gold disk, with a strange looking arrow that was opened into two halves. Fellon would surely find this of interest!

He searched halfheartedly for a few more minutes for Nicky's body. Then rose to his feet. He heard another rumble. The mine was fast becoming extremely unstable. Now, he would return to the Fortress and tell his master that the boy was buried in the mine, but he had recovered the gold object.

Fellon did not know Nicky also had the Key, and Shredd would not tell him that piece of information.

He sent a message to Tarr and Dreygon, not knowing the latter was no more. *Retrieve the captured Fae-rens and return to the Fortress. He had recovered what Fellon the Cursed wanted.*

CHAPTER 20

# LEAVING WREN

The Grand One gave her pterodactyl guard and Kendar last instructions for guarding Wren while she was traveling to the underground hiding place of the Altar of Hope. She also needed a group of Protector Fae-rens to be look-outs to hinder or stop any evil from following her. The ruler sent out a telepathic message calling one hundred Protector Fae-rens to assemble outside of the sanctuary.

In less than two minutes, the Protectors lined up. Brem-mer, now without a mate and not a strong as the mated Fae-rens, also lined-up. Glymirra, seeing this, understood his intention and let him stay. She began to address the group like soldiers.

"My Protectors, we have been doing our best to keep

the living safe on Gaeya, even with the instability caused by the the lost Key. I know you have heard that our brave, new Guardian, under extreme danger, has returned the Elka, the Key of Healing and Rebirth, to me. It has been lost for too many years causing Gaeya's strange climate and conditions to rapidly deteriorate, feeding the evil. It created Fellon and his more powerful dark ones to threaten all the living and more recently our world, Wren.

"I need to journey as quickly as possible to the Altar of Hope and unite all four Keys of Being. I now ask you to risk your lives once more to help me move safely to the secret entrance. Divide up into groups of ten. You must take the winds to the north, to the south, to the east and west in a ten-mile radius. Keep me informed of the locations of any dark presence." As the group of Fae-rens crossed their right fists over the left side of their chest and bowed.

Glymirra spread her majestic wings, ascending into the sky. With a swish of her hands, she cloaked her appearance and disappeared from sight. The small legion of Protector Fae-rens followed.

Many of the animals and worker Fae-rens in Wren

looked up. It was rare to see their ruler leave Wren, but news of the return of the Elka had all in good spirits. The threats of the evil entering this realm now would not come true. Joining the four Keys of Being would finally set the balance and weaken the Cursed One and his followers. Soon, normalcy would return to the inner realm.

But less than thirty seconds into her flight, the Grand One received an emergency message: the gold opulan that Nicky had dropped outside the portal was gone.

No trace of it was found. Only the cold frost left by an evil entity remained.

.